Found

A NOVEL

NIKKI ANNE SCHMUTZ

THOMSON PRODUCTIONS

THOMSON PRODUCTIONS
1-800-226-0155

Cover design by Greg Thomas

Manufactured in the United States

ACKNOWLEDGEMENTS

I would like to thank my husband, Richard. Without his encouragement and support this book would have never been finished. I could not ask for a better husband and father.

Thanks to Debbie Thomas, my mother. You have always been there for me. Thanks for taking care of my children and never doubting this could be done. Thanks to my dad, Nick Thomas, who gave me a foundation on which to draw from. Thank you Shannon, Carrie, Richard, Stephanie, Sam, & Jake for loving your big sister. Thank you Grandma Norlyene Harding for the excitement you exhibit in what I am doing and for loving me. You give so much, thank you.

Thanks to Stan Jr., Bobi, Joey, & Dawn Schmutz. Stanton & Joyce Schmutz and the whole Schmutz Clan. Steve & Laura Thomas and rest the extended Thomas family. And all of you Harding's. You never ceased to encourage and believe.

Thanks to Greg Thomas for assisting in formatting and designing the cover of this book, it's beautiful.

Thanks to Ruth Schmutz who generously edited and proof-read this book. Your insights and corrections are vital to the success of this book. And to Bethany Cory who also proofread, you are a great friend.

Thank you Linda Thomson for never doubting that I could pull it off. You have always believed in me and I love you.

But most of all, I wish to thank God. Without Him none of this would have been possible. He is my light, my life, my everything. It is He that has blessed me with this story.

FOR RICHARD...

You are the reason I have begun to heal.

Thank you my love...

CONTENTS

PROLOGUE
Leaving Home
May 25th

"No!" boomed the deep voice of Charles Stately. "I will not have you ruining the reputation of this family! Not any more!" He grabbed Samantha's arm and forced her out of the front hall and into his study. Samantha had meant to run to her room. She wanted to escape, to get away from it all. She knew what she had done was wrong. She didn't need her father harping on her once again.

Behind them, Lorna ushered two policemen out the front door, then shut it tight and leaned against it. She wanted to rescue her daughter from the wrath of her husband. But she couldn't. His wrath would turn to her. She quietly walked to the door of the study, poked her head around the corner, and listened.

Samantha sat on the red leather chair facing a large mahogany desk. Book shelves filled with leather bound editions lined the walls. It was a regal room. Charles stood next to Samantha, looking as if he would attack at any second. There was anger in his brown eyes. Lorna had seen that anger before, many times before.

"What were you thinking?" Charles demanded harshly, taking a step forward.

"We were just having fun..." Samantha began defiantly.

"Fun?" Charles called out incredulously. "Is there a brain in your head or have you wasted it away with all of your fun? Your behavior is unacceptable! I will not have it in this house! Our family is a pillar in the community. We will act as such."

"Yea, a pillar. Not if they knew how you treated us." Samantha shot back, her voice rising to a high pitch shout. "You've never been a pillar to me! You don't even care about me!"

"You say that after all I've done for you! After all I've given you!" His face flushed red with anger.

"I don't want any of it! The price is too high. I'd rather be on my own than have to live up to your unreal expectations."

"You are an ungrateful child! You are not worth my time." Charles raved. "You are nothing!"

Tears stung at Samantha's eyes. There it was again. Her father thought nothing of her. It hadn't mattered what she had ever done to try to please him. He had never been pleased. So she had stopped trying.

Samantha looked her father squarely in his eyes. She searched for the slightest bit of concern, the smallest acknowledgement that he cared about her. It wasn't there. She turned around and ran up the curved staircase to the second floor, down the hall and into her room. She slammed her door. The sound reverberated through the house.

"Go get your gown on. We have a party starting in an hour." Charles said to Lorna through tight lips. Lorna hesitated before turning away. She wanted to talk to Charles about their daughter. No matter what she said Charles would see it as Lorna taking Samantha's side. Why did it always have to be that way? Lorna sighed and made her way to her bedroom to ready herself for the evening. She hesitated at her door. Samantha's door was shut. She wanted to go to her, to wrap her arms around her only daughter and apologize for Charles' actions. But it wouldn't do any good. They were empty words. Charles wasn't sorry and both of them knew it.

~

Samantha lay on her bed, face down and cried until the wee hours of the morning. Why couldn't her father love her? Why didn't God love her? God used to be someone she trusted. Now He seemed like a myth, a story that she had heard long ago. He was Halleluiah praises, angels, and heaven. Nothing she considered to be real.

All Samantha knew was the story of her family and what they had evolved into. The once close knitted threesome were church attending socialites. Her father spent time with her. He loved her. Over the years he had changed. Her father was now a prominent member of the community, a Wall Street tycoon, who worshipped money and all it could bring.

Lorna had watched her husband change, not knowing what to do. She was afraid of losing him. She couldn't stand up to him; she couldn't stand up for herself. There was no trace of what had once brought her parents together. They were not happy. Lorna cheered her daughter in her successes and urged her to do as her father asked. Samantha had decided that she would not give in and become a hollow being, like her mother had.

She would not live her life that way. And now this. Being escorted home by the police tonight had only been a minor problem compared to what Samantha needed to tell them.

Her father had told her, in no uncertain terms, that because of her defiance she was a disgrace to the family, a mark that maybe, just maybe, could be covered if Samantha did no more disgraceful things.

But she did. And this time it was something that she could not cover up. She was pregnant and the father refused to accept any responsibility.

Samantha had meant to tell her parents about the baby, but her young mind came to a realization.

If she told, her father would disown her. The very thought brought new tears to Samantha's eyes and a plan formed in her mind.

She would leave. She would runway, have the baby and come back later. Her parents wouldn't know what had taken place, and Samantha would never tell them. Facing the wrath of disappearing would be better than the truth. Some black marks could be easily covered, others last a lifetime.

The next morning, after her father had left for work; Samantha packed a few belongings in a backpack. She quietly walked down the halls, past the extra bedrooms, up the stairs to the third floor. The house was cluttered with half filled wine glasses, trays covered in crumbs, and rumpled chairs left by guests the night before.

Gingerly she tiptoed into her Mother's room. Lorna lay haphazardly across the king-size bed; passed out from the liquor her husband drove her to drink. Samantha crossed the room and opened the hand-carved mahogany jewelry box that graced the top of the dresser. Her hand grasped a wad of tightly wound bills. It was her mother's liquor stash. There was no other way she would be able to escape. Samantha thrust it into her pocket and retreated.

"Goodbye, Mom..." Samantha whispered.

As she went to close the door something caught her eye.

On her mother's nightstand was a book. It was old, the pages were yellowed, and the red leather binding had come apart from wear. It was one of Mother's most prized possessions. Often Samantha had seen her mother reading it, usually with tears in her eyes. It was a journal of some kind.

Samantha grabbed the book and stuffed it into her bag as she left the room. She wasn't sure why she took it. Perhaps because she knew she would miss her mother and wanted to have something of hers. Or perhaps Samantha just wanted to take something that she loved away from her mother. Either way, Samantha felt she needed that book.

She did not look back as she calmly walked away from the house she called home. Samantha was a mixture of feelings. Relief flowed through her as she realized she would not have to face her father about the pregnancy. Her steps felt light and the usual heaviness upon her shoulders was gone. She was free! She felt like she could do anything!

But a sense of dread lingered just beneath the surface. Samantha had no idea where she would go.

CHAPTER ONE
Lost and Almost Dead
December 5th

The night was cold. The trees and light posts lining the Chicago streets were coated with a layer of ice. A bitter wind whisked around Samantha, piercing the layers of her clothing and striking frost down to her bones. Her swollen feet hurt with each step and her back ached from the weight of her round stomach.

What was she doing? She should go home. But, she couldn't. Not after all this time. She had spent six months living on the street. Going home now would defeat the very purpose of her flight.

But, what would she do? Her stomach groaned and the familiar nausea set in. She needed to eat. Thanksgiving Day and a few more had passed without any scraps of food to be found.

Samantha thought of Thanksgiving.

If she had been home she would have dined in the great hall, dressed in a formal her mother would have bought for her. A string quartet would have sat in the corner, accompanying the meal. Friends and family would have sat around the large table, talking of politics and art as they ate the feast off of the gold rimmed china only used on special occasions.

The food would have been delicious. Kelly, the head chef, would have spent days on the feast. The buffet table would be lined with food. There would be the largest turkey they could find. Then there would be mounds of whipped potatoes, a ham, and all kinds of salads, shrimp, caviar, and wine. Her parents would have let her drink one glass of wine

The dress, the parties... it was all for keeping up the appearances. When her father wasn't trying to impress anyone his true feelings came out. He was a bitter man, bent on the fact that the world was taking advantage of him at every turn.

To top it off his only daughter was a disgrace to the Stately name. How could she party with her friends, and get caught! Under age drinkers! What else had she gotten mixed-up in? Drugs?

Her mind wandered to her 'adventures', as she called them. There had been drugs, but only a sample. And yes there was more than her share of alcohol and shoplifting... Her father chalked it all up to a rebellious teenage girl, choosing the wrong things.

Just once she would have like to point out that she needed a family. She needed their love and support. If they had been there for her maybe she would have turned out better. It was too late now. The damage had already been done. She couldn't take back what she had done any easier than her father could mend his own actions over the last five years.

Samantha didn't regret leaving.

She had not left a single clue as to where she had gone. Not a note, not a phone call. There had not been a single sighting of her for six months.

Deep down she had hoped that they would have tried to find her. They had enough money to launch a nation-wide search. And yet nothing had happened. Usually the disappearance of a wealthy family's child caught wind in the press. It hadn't.

She was sure they hadn't even reported her missing. That was what hurt more than anything else. They didn't care.

So, it was for the best that she didn't tell them. Finding out that their only daughter was pregnant would have been the beginning of the end of their family. She would have this baby and give it up. There was no way she could take care of it alone and she wouldn't take it home. Her child deserved a family, a home, a life worth living.

Another blast of wind, from off the lakefront, almost knocked her over. She steadied herself against a building.

First she had gone to New York City. After having no luck finding anyone that would hire her and realizing that her parents were not looking for her, she found her way to Chicago. For some reason she had believed in her heart that the farther away she got from her parents, the better things would be. Chicago seemed as good a place as any to go to. But she had been wrong.

Things were worse here in the Windy City.

It was well past midnight. She had waited in her usual alley just off Michigan Avenue, until after the fancy restaurant closed and everyone left. Then, she awkwardly climbed into the dumpster. At the end of the day they would throw out the unused food. If she got there quick it wouldn't be too bad.

That's how she had survived.

Here in Chicago she had tried to get a job, but no one wanted to hire a pregnant sixteen year old who had no address or phone number to list on the application. There was no one to go to, no one to call in case of emergency.

Tonight was colder than usual and the air smelled like snow. She had to find somewhere to sleep, somewhere warm.

She scrounged together enough change along the side-walk to ride the 'L' and took the Evanston Express, north out of town. The city was so cold.

Her lungs felt heavy and her breathing was labored. The backpack on her back seemed to weigh her down.

Evanston was a nice suburb, nestled against Lake Michigan. Upon arrival, Samantha walked down the street from the station. She had no idea where she was going. She was tired and hoped that a better situation would present itself. She hoped she would find a good place to sleep soon.

As the night wore on her thoughts became less and less coherent. Strange fragments of thoughts and memories crowded her mind like pieces of fabric in a mismatched patchwork quilt, except nothing fit together.

Snow began to fall from the sky, tiny flakes of crystals sparkling against the darkness.

Samantha's feet shuffled against the sidewalk, leaving prolonged tracks in the film of soft white flakes. Soon she didn't know how far she had walked, what time it was, nor did her mind recall where she was. Only one thing resounded in her frozen body, sleep... sleep...

Out of the fragments of thoughts a vivid memory of a woman she had met out on the street in New York came to the surface. Samantha had been asking for money when the woman approached her. "Turn to God." The woman had said. "If you pray to Him, He will help you." Samantha had just passed it off as some religion hyped person who thought prayer could fix anything. Now Samantha wondered.

Would a prayer really help? She had grown up saying her prayers at night before going to bed. Had that made a difference? She wasn't sure. All she knew was that her family no longer practiced religion and they were not any happier for it. Prayer was worth a try, Samantha decided.

"God.... If you're there... I ..... can't ...walk.......help..." Her foot slid with her next step, causing her to fall to the ground. It took every ounce of strength to pick herself up. As she did, she almost slipped again. Her body trembled.

In the distance was a bright light.

A church on the next corner stood against the dark-ened sky. In front, on what was the lawn area was a well-lit stable. Inside stood a life-size Joseph and Mary looking down into the face of their newborn son, Jesus.

A strange warmness filled her heart. The almost inco-herent girl stumbled forward until she reached the figures. She fell to her knees in front of baby Jesus.

Her tears flowed easily. Her trembling hand reached in and caressed the cheek of the babe lying in the manger.

"Hello... baby... Jesus." Samantha looked up at Mary with squinted eyes. "I'm... having... a baby... too." Her hands immediately went to her stomach. It was well rounded. Though she didn't know how far along she was, she felt there wasn't much time left.

The love she felt melted into anger. Life wasn't fair! Samantha threw herself down on the hay that was covered with a light dusting of snow.

"If there's... a God... why do things... like this... hap-pen?" She looked up into the dark sky. Snow swirled down as if heaven were dumping it out onto the world. It almost seemed like a sign.

There was no love up there. God wasn't there.

"If you're... real.... than my... family.... would have... loved... me! I'm... alone."

The feelings that flowed through her body, her emotions, became too much for her. Just before she slipped out of consciousness Samantha realized that she did feel something. Maybe God really was up there after all.

CHAPTER TWO
Marion's Awakening
Middle of the Night

Sixty year-old Marion Mahoney awoke with a start. She felt the other side of the bed for her husband. It was empty.

Then she remembered.

He was gone to the Christian Minister's Conference in Tennessee. He would be back Saturday night.

She looked at the clock on her cherry wood night-stand. 2:35 a.m., it read in bright red numbers.

As the haze of sleep dispersed, Marion became keenly aware of the feeling that had awoken her. Her gut twisted in apprehension. Her palms were sweating. No dream had plagued her sleep.

She knew this feeling.

She had felt this way before, when either her husband or one of her children had been in danger. Thoughts of her children raced through her mind.

They had all been at her house for Thanksgiving a few days ago and had traveled back to their own homes. Jesse, her oldest, lived in Colorado with his wife and four children. Teresa lived in Tulsa with her husband and the twins. Justin was going to graduate school in Chicago. Her youngest, Marie was newly wed and lived a few minutes away in Skokie.

The feeling returned like a wave washing over her senses. Anything could have gone wrong with one of them, or even her husband. What was it?

Marion closed her eyes and focused inside herself. After having this type of feeling so many times over the past forty years, she had learned to decipher the meaning, to pin point the exact reason of the apprehension. She knew that God spoke to everyone; most people just didn't know how to hear him.

No, it wasn't any of them. It was something else.

Marion pushed the down comforter off her legs and got out of bed. As she stood she slipped on her fuzzy house slippers. Her wrinkled hands grabbed a pink terry cloth bathrobe hanging by the door. She threw it on over her flower print flannel night gown as she walked down the hall of the home she had lived in for the past thirty years, and into the kitchen. It was a small home, but it had been adequate for the needs of her family.

With trembling fingers she flipped on the light, crossed the room, and reached for a glass in the cupboard.

A drink of water was what she needed.

As she filled up the glass with water from the tap the feeling whooshed through her body once again, this time stronger than before. She dropped the glass into the porcelain sink, shattering it into thousands of tiny pieces.

Someone was in trouble. Real trouble.

Marion lifted her eyes, looking out the window. The storm was heavy; almost blinding snow caused the chapel next door to look as if it simply was not there. It was just her, in her house, in a wilderness of white washed stormy sky.

But the old church was there, just like it had been for a quarter of a century.

She went to turn away from the window, but something stopped her. It was as if a voice had whispered to her.

Look again!

Marion peered out, following the prompting. Her hazel eyes scanned the area, back and forth. It was no use. Even with her good vision the storm was too heavy to see more than a few feet from the house.

She squeezed her eyes shut and clasped her hands together against her chest as she leaned her old body against the cold kitchen counter.

"Father in Heaven, if thou wilt have me help thou shall have to lift the storm for a moment so I may see what is out there." Marion prayed out loud. Members of the congregation had always admired the amount of faith the Reverend's wife displayed. When they would ask her about acquiring such faith Marion would simply reply that if they truly put their lives into God's hands, He would make himself manifest in more ways then they had ever imagined.

Marion finished her prayer and waited for the familiar warm feeling that always accompanied an answer to questions.

A sweet peace flowed into her mind, quieting the uneasiness. She allowed her eyes to open and again peered out the window.

Marion waited for God to show her. She squinted her eyes, and then leaned forward. She could not see anything past the blinding flurry of dancing flakes.

Then, like a curtain had been drawn, the falling snow parted in a direct path, to the Manger scene Marion had set up the day before. Like Moses parting the Red Sea, God had given Marion the answer to her prayer.

At the foot of the manger was a dark mound.

Immediately after Marion recognized the mound as the reason for her feelings, the storm swirled back in, enveloping the once clearly outlined path. As if in rebellion to the miracle, the falling snow thickened with a vengeance.

Marion's eyes widened in amazement as her lips uttered a prayer of thanks. God had granted her a miracle, like he had so many times before. This was what she had been looking for, she was sure of it.

Marion's heart nearly pounded right out of her chest as she raced out the back door, paying no attention to the fact that she was not dressed to go outside.

The heavy gusts of snow whipped around her and she pulled at her robe trying to keep it securely about her wrinkled body. The snowflakes were flying so fast it stung as they slapped at her face. She squinted her eyes, trying to see.

It was no use.

The minutes it took to reach the nativity seemed like forever to Marion, but finally she was there.

She did not notice the icy wetness seeping through her house slippers.

Timidly she approached, afraid that it might be some kind of animal that needed help. She did not want to alarm it.

On the ground, covered with a thin layer of snow was the mound. Marion reached her hand out, slowly, nervously. She grabbed at what she found to be fabric and gently pulled it away.

The face of a young girl lay beneath. Marion gasped. She shook the girl gently.

Nothing.

With a firm hand Marion rolled the girl over. The face looking up at her seemed vaguely familiar, but Marion couldn't place where she had seen it before. The girl's features were slender. Her white skin was contrasted by the mess of dark hair that tumbled out from the hood of her coat. Having a husband as a minister, she had been involved in helping many people over the years. Had this girl been a member of the congregation?

Snowflakes landed on the girl's face, sticking to her frozen lashes. Her lips were slightly blue. Marion leaned her ear in, listening for breath.

She was alive!

Knowing what she had to do Marion said yet another prayer.

"Oh Lord, give me the strength to carry this girl."

Using all the strength she could muster, Marion pulled the girl up and across her frail shoulders, in a fireman's carry, and slowly, painfully made her way through the snow towards her house.

The snow was blinding. If Marion hadn't known the way so well, she would have been in trouble. She lost her way only once, but corrected her path when she ran into the line of bushes bordering her front lawn.

With heavy steps she made it up to the back door, opened it, and heaved the girl inside. She managed to get her into the living room where she dropped the girl's limp body on the sofa.

Marion stepped back. The moment of strength passed, leaving her with waves of tiredness and weak muscles that threatened to give way from beneath her.

The room swirled around her. She did not have the strength to carry this girl as she had. She knew the strength had only come from one place.

The Almighty God had sent it.

For reasons she didn't understand, she was meant to help this girl.

~

After phoning a long time friend and neighbor, who was a doctor, Marion set about the task of getting the wet clothes off the girl. Her old muscles weren't what they used to be. They screamed out in pain as she lifted the girl again and again. She should have waited for help.

But she couldn't.

Once a long time ago she had been in a similar situation and it had been embarrassing to know that the doctor had changed her clothes. She would not allow that to happen to this girl.

As Marion pulled the heavy, mud-encrusted coat away, she stopped abruptly. Her eyes widened. The thin girls' stomach protruded out, large and round.

She was pregnant.

For a moment, Marion could not breathe. Her ears began to ring, her stomach quivered. With a shake of her head, she quickly pulled herself together.

Once the dry, ill-fitting pajamas that belonged to her husband were in place Marion grabbed a large quilt from the hall closet and lay it over the girls' body.

There had been a backpack on the girl's back, under-neath her coat. Marion was tempted to look inside, to find the identity of the girl.

She didn't. She would wait.

What had happened to this poor young thing? Marion had no idea how she had gotten in her churchyard. Or why she was out in the middle of a stormy night like this one.

All Marion knew was that she would do anything to help her.

CHAPTER THREE
The Doctor Arrives
Three a.m.

"I'd say she's got a bad case of malnutrition, along with severe chest congestion." stated the old Doctor, Ted Burns, as he buckled up the large black bag. His heavy overcoat had been thrown over a nearby chair after his arrival. He was dressed for a house call, dress shirt and bow tie. His eyes showed signs of sleep. His gray hair was slightly ruffled.

"Oh, Ted! The poor thing..." Marion folded her arms against her, feeling the softness of her bathrobe. It had been a gift from her husband.

Deep lines of worry surrounded her eyes as Marion looked at the girl.

She lay still, color finally returning to her cheeks, a slight blue tinge still was showing at her lips. Marion looked up at Dr. Burns, then back to the girl. He spoke quietly.

"She might need to go to the hospital. Let's wait until morning to see how she's doing. I don't know how well that baby will be when it's born. I'd guess that she's about seven or eight months along."

They both stood there, in silence, eyes riveted on the girl. The doctor finally broke the silence.

"I'll call in the morning, Marion." He let himself out as he had so many times before.

Marion stood there, watching the girl.

Her features were delicate. Long dark brown hair fell in tangled piles beside her face. Her eyes were framed with thick lashes. Her fingers were long.

Piano fingers, Marion mused.

All of her own children had been blessed with long slender fingers, perfect for piano playing. She had taught every one of them how to play.

The girl seemed tall and was deathly skinny. Her large stomach seemed out of place.

Marion bent to retrieve the dirty clothes that lay at the foot of the couch. The girl had been wearing four layers of clothing. She would throw them in the washing machine, and then assess if they were worth keeping. The tag on the coat caught her eye.

Tommy Hilfiger.

Not a brand of clothing a teenager in trouble usually had.

~

Marion's body protested as she started the washing machine at the back of the house. One scoop of laundry detergent, a little bleach, and her sore hands stuffed the clothes inside. She closed the lid.

She shut the laundry room door, hoping the noise of the machine would not disturb the girl and crawled back into her cold bed.

The clock read 4:23 a.m.

She was exhausted, but she knew sleep would not come easily. Tonight was a night of mysteries and her mind wanted to solve them. But that was not all. She was remembering.

She had been lost once.

She wouldn't dwell on the past; it only brought the familiar heartache that she had never been able to bandage. But after seeing the girl, it had all come back to her.

Marion groaned.

"It's been more than forty years ago!" She slapped at the pillow next to her. "Get over it old woman!" She chastened herself. There had been many other times when the memories were unearthed in her mind. But for a reason she couldn't understand, tonight it was worse than she ever remembered.

Marion clicked the lamp on at the side of her bed and sat up.

How could she sleep? She needed her husband. He understood the past that plagued her. He was the only one that could console her.

No. That wasn't true.

God had always been there for her, even when she thought he had abandoned her for good, that she wasn't worthy of His divine intervention.

Marion knelt at the side of her bed.

"Dear God, I thank thee for this opportunity of service thou hast sent me. I am thy servant, O Lord. Please give me the strength to endure. Please bless me with the inspiration to know what to do, how to help this young girl..."

As Marion climbed back into bed a peace swept over her. She fell asleep with the knowledge that God was there. He was directing the course of her life, and He was ready to help her overcome her own painful past.

CHAPTER FOUR
First Impressions
December 6th

Samantha Lorna Stately tried to open her eyes. They fluttered open, and then closed again. She felt warm and safe. That was a feeling she hadn't felt since leaving home. Samantha tried to recall where she had bedded down for the night and could not. She took a deep breath and coughed.

Where was she?

She pushed her eyes open and looked around. She lay on a burgundy colored couch. A large fluffy rainbow patterned quilt covered her and a soft down pillow lay under her head.

It was a living room.

On either side of the door leading outside were curio cabinets. Bookcases lined one wall; formal sitting chairs with a small table between them lined another. The table housed a flower arrangement and a statue of Jesus with long hair, wearing a robe. There were two sheep at his side. The walls were papered with a cheery flower pattern. Beautiful paintings hung here and there. A nice chandelier hung from the ceiling over the couch on which she lay. The floor was a shiny wood. A large area rug covered the center of the room. The couch faced a fireplace where a small fire glowed. A Christmas tree twinkled with white and red lights. Behind her was a door she assumed led to the rest of the home.

A slight movement within brought a smile to her face. Her baby...

A coughing attack overtook her body. She grasped at her chest burning with pain as she tried to stop the barks that came from her.

Marion heard the coughs from the kitchen where she was preparing breakfast. She raced to the sink, grabbed a glass of water, and scurried to the front room.

There, bent forward in sitting position, was the girl. Her body racked with each cough and Marion was afraid that she might crumble at the force of each cough that erupted from the girl's small frame.

Marion walked into the room and put a warm hand on the girl's shoulder.

At the touch, Samantha jumped. She had not seen anyone enter. She looked up into warm blue-green eyes, surrounded by wrinkles.

Another coughing fit came.

Marion raised the glass, urging the girl to take a drink.

Samantha sat up and took it, thankfully. Her body ached and the glass seemed heavy. She drank. Coughed again. Then drank once more. The cool water soothed her throat. She took another drink, than lay back against the pillow. The coughing had taken all of her energy.

Marion watched the girl close her eyes and take a few deep breaths before she reached out and took the glass from the girl's trembling hand. After a few moments the girl's eyes opened once again. Marion spoke softly.

"Hello. My name is Marion. I found you outside last night and brought you in." Marion explained, hoping that the girl was not afraid.

"Hi..." was all Samantha said. Her mind reeled at the thought. Someone had found her? Where was she?

Then it all came back to her. Wandering, falling, being so cold, praying, and talking to Baby Jesus. Samantha closed her eyes, remembering that she felt as if her life had been over. And she was sure that if she hadn't been found, it would have been.

This woman had found her?

"How are you feeling dear?" Marion asked as she tugged one of the chairs from the other side of the room over and faced it towards the couch and sat down. She watched the girl intently.

"I hurt all over." Samantha said carefully as she studied the woman. She was old. Her shoulders slumped forward slightly, arching her back out. Her gray hair was curled against her head in the style that so many grandmothers wore their hair. She wore a long-sleeved pink button-up shirt and black slacks.

"I don't feel very good at all. But my baby is kicking." Samantha volunteered.

Marion smiled. This girl was conscious of the child within her.

"What is your name, dear?" Marion asked gently.

Samantha tightened at the question. Living out on the street you had to be careful who you knew your name. Everyone was out to use you. She looked up at the old woman who called herself Marion and into her trusting, caring eyes.

"Samantha." She said simply.

"I always liked that name." Marion said as she remembered deciding what she would name her first girl. Samantha had been one of her choices. Marion could tell that the girl did not want to say much. Understanding that time would build trust, Marion decided that a little hot soup might give the girl some strength.

"I've made some soup, I'll go get it."

~

After presenting Samantha with a bowl of homemade chicken noodle soup, Marion went to the study and called Doctor Burns. He said he would visit within the hour.

"Samantha," Marion said as she returned to the front room. "I've got a good doctor friend who is coming to check on you. He was also here last night, making sure you were all right. I'll let you rest until he gets here." Marion pulled the doors closed between the front room and the hall and left Samantha to rest.

When Samantha was finished eating, she placed the bowl on the narrow table behind the sofa and snuggled back into the quilt.

Suddenly her heart leapt with fear! Feeling this warmth was something she knew would not last. Now that she had been taken in she might be turned in. That was something she could not have!

Her parents could not know about the baby. She would do all she could to avoid it! She needed to get out of here!

Samantha spotted her backpack at the foot of the couch and grabbed it, ready to flee for her life. Within seconds her weak hands dropped the bag. She did not have the energy to leave. The realization heightened the sense of urgency. What would she do?

She could no nothing, at least not until she felt a little better. For now she would rest. She needed the rest.

CHAPTER FIVE
Assessment of Health
A Little Later...

Doctor Burns arrived within the hour, allowing Samantha to take a short nap. She awoke when the bell at the front door rang.

Marion rushed into the room and let the doctor inside.

He was a tall man, broad-shouldered, and strong for his seventy-years. He smiled at Samantha.

"Well, good morning!" He deposited a black bag on the table and pulled out a stethoscope. He listened to her heart, her lungs, and the baby. He took her blood pressure, temperature, and even a sample of blood. He then handed her a pile of pills, instructing her to take them. She did.

Samantha realized she was wearing pajamas that she had never seen before. She wanted to ask the old woman if she had changed her clothes.

But, Samantha said nothing, fearing they would ask why she had been out in the snow, almost dead.

But they didn't.

At the end of his exam, Doctor Burns looked Samantha in the eye.

"Young Lady. You are a very sick girl. You'll get better,

31

and your baby will live, if you do all Marion says. She's a good woman." He paused and raised his finger. "You do what she says or I'll put you in the hospital." His eyes did not leave hers until Samantha nodded in agreement. "I'll get this blood tested, and return the results soon." He said to both of them.

"Thanks Ted, I really appreciate it." Marion said as she let him out.

Samantha watched them go. She leaned back, completely worn out from the examination. She willed herself to relax. Wondering if they would question her caused the muscles in her shoulders to clench up.

Marion stepped back into the house, closed the door tight, and took a deep breath. It was time to ask questions.

"Is there anyone I should call for you?" Marion inquired as she sat down on the chair. This girl must have someone that would want to know of her illness, someone who would take care of her.

Samantha looked away not knowing what to say. She pursed her lips together.

"Do you have a family, or friends...?"

"I don't have a family." Samantha interrupted with her weak voice. "I'm all alone." She nervously shifted the quilt around her, hugging it against her middle.

It was the truth, Samantha inwardly defended.

"You have no one?" Marion asked carefully, sensing the girl wasn't telling the truth. Then again, maybe she was. There were many homeless, orphaned children in the world.

"No one. I've been on my own for awhile."

"How have you survived?" Marion wondered how a pregnant girl would have faired on her own. Obviously she had not faired very well. She was quite ill.

"I've managed." Samantha stated softly. Part of her wanted to trust this woman. Why was that? She didn't even know her.

Marion wondered how to get this girl to open up to her. She uttered a silent prayer and closed her eyes for a moment. Then, a flash of inspiration came.

"Alright. You don't know anything about me and I don't know anything about you. How about we play a game? You ask me a question that I'll answer, and then I'll do the same to you. If you don't want to answer it then don't. Is that fair enough?" Marion watched as the girl's face softened and knew that it would work. "You go first."

Samantha watched Marion for a moment. What could it hurt? She didn't have to answer, right?

"Do you have a husband?"

"Yes. He is away until tomorrow at a conference. He's the minister for the church next door." Samantha thought of the cold and empty building as she had seen it last

33

night. To know that this nice woman attended there warmed her in some way.

"Do you have a mother and father?" Marion asked.

"Yes." There were a few moments of silence. "Do you have any kids?"

"Yes. As a matter of fact, I have four. They have all grown up and moved out." Marion answered. "Do your parents know where you are?" she continued.

"No." Samantha said, hot tears coming to her eyes. She quickly blinked them away. "Did you change my clothes?"

"Yes, I did it all by myself. Those pajamas you are wearing are my husband's." Samantha felt much better knowing that no one else, especially the doctor had been there when her wet clothes had been taken off.

"Do you like dogs?" Samantha asked.

"Yes. Though I have never had one of my own. I'm allergic to them," said Marion with a smile. Samantha smiled too.

"I'm allergic to dogs too." Samantha's eyes drooped. Marion could tell she was tired. The medicine the doctor had left would make her sleepy. It was beginning to take effect.

"Samantha. I won't do anything that you don't want me to do." Marion tried to assure her. "I am only here to help. You can stay in my home until we figure out a place for you to live permanently, but I need to talk openly about your family and why you are not with them. It will help me understand why you are all alone." Samantha looked down at the floor deciding what to say. She shook her head as she answered.

"They don't care." The words seemed harsh, even to Samantha's own ears, but she believed them.

There was a long pause.

"What will you do with your baby?" Marion asked, hoping Samantha would not become defensive.

"I want to give it up." Samantha said with conviction. "I want it to have a family, a real family." Samantha's words revealed more than she realized.

Marion heard more than a wish for an unborn child. She heard an admission. Her family was not 'real'. That could mean just about anything. Marion wanted to ask more about her family, but decided against it. Whatever this young girl had gone through stemmed from her family. Not wanting to push her too far, Marion stopped the questions.

"The medicine is making you sleepy. You rest, and call out if you need anything." Marion made sure that Samantha's drink was where she could reach it, and then left her alone.

Samantha was tired.

She was relieved that the old woman didn't ask any

more questions. At the same time, she realized that she wanted to tell her more. Maybe this woman could help her. Maybe she should tell her everything.

Samantha's head hurt.

As she trailed off to sleep, she thought of her life and how this was the first time, in a long time, that she felt cared for and safe.

CHAPTER SIX
The Reverend Returns
December 7th

The next morning Marion cleaned the house thoroughly. It wasn't very messy, but she wanted it sparkling by the time her husband returned home.

Samantha slept all day, never calling out in need of anything.

Marion made sure Samantha's medication was taken on time and that she ate to keep up her strength.

Few words were passed between the two.

Samantha was too tired to talk, and she wasn't sure what to say to the kind old woman. Her ravaged body could do little more than eat and sleep and Marion let her.

At ten after four, Marion called Marie, asking her to go pick up her father from the airport at six. Marie agreed, but was concerned. Nothing less than an emergency would pull her mother away from being the first person to see her husband after being away from him.

Marion assured her that everything was all right. She was caring for a sick teenage girl and didn't feel she could leave her with someone else.

After hanging up the phone, Marion set to the task of making dinner. She prepared a roast, surrounded it with onions, potatoes, and carrots, and put it in the oven.

At six-thirty she went in to check on Samantha. She was still sleeping.

Marion retired to her room to rest for a few minutes.

~

The sound of the back door signaled the arrival of her husband. With joy in her heart, Marion ran to the kitchen.

Just inside the back door, taking off his coat, was Reverend James Mahoney.

He was a tall man, his lean frame accentuated by his shoulders. Despite his sixty-two years, his hair was still dark, only beginning to gray at his temples. His eyes were blue and had a way of looking into people's very soul.

Marion's heart still leaped at the sight of him. They had so many good years to look back on.

"James!" She went to him, throwing her arms around his waist fiercely.

"Marion..." they held each other tight, until they were interrupted by the back door opening once again.

Marie entered, carrying a small pile of paperback books.

"Hey, you two... I can't even get into the house if you don't move out of the way." Marie said with a laugh. The Mahoney children were used to the displays of affection shown between their parents.

With arms around each other James and Marion walked to the kitchen where James deposited his carry-on bag on the floor next to the oak dining table.

"Mother, I brought these books for your visitor. I thought maybe she needed something to do." Marie set them down on the table, her short dark hair bouncing. She was a younger version of Marion with her dark hair and bright eyes, though Marion's hair was now gray.

"Thank you. I'm sure that when she is feeling better, she will enjoy them." Marion met James's eyes. Obviously Marie had told him what little she knew about the girl. Through the years they had brought many people in need within the walls of their home and James trusted Marion's judgment without question.

"So, who is she?" Marie asked eagerly as she sat up to the table.

"Her name is Samantha." Marion said, knowing full well that if the girl was awake, she was probably listening. "She's pregnant and in trouble."

Marie, too, was used to her parents helping others. That was how she had lived her life, in service of her fellow men.

When her mother didn't volunteer any more information, Marie knew it wasn't time to talk.

She raised her arm and looked at her watch.

"It smells good in here, but I've got to get dinner ready

for Trevor. I'll call you tomorrow." With that she hurried out the same way she had come in.

The kitchen was left in a comfortable silence.

James had never been a man of many words. He was kind, and full of wisdom. Marion looked up at him. His eyes were closed.

He looked tired.

"Dinner is ready. Let me get you a plate." Marion offered. James took his bag to the bedroom and washed up.

By the time he circled back to the kitchen, there were two steamy hot plates of food adorning the table.

They took their seats, next to each other on one side, and prayed before they began to eat.

"The food is wonderful, Marion. Thank you." James said between bites.

"You're welcome." Marion said in return. James had always been good at showing his appreciation.

"Where is our guest?" James asked. His long arm reached across the table, grabbing the salt.

"She is asleep on the sofa in the front room." Marion told him. They had an extra bedroom, but at the moment it was filled with projects for the Christmas Party they were having at the church in two weeks.

"I trust you called Doctor Burns."

"I did, the very night I found her." Marion said. She recalled how she had found Samantha.

"That fact that I found her at all was a miracle." Marion took a deep breath.

"Tell me." James said. He took one last bite and placed his fork to the side of his plate. He folded his arms in front of him, ready to listen.

"Two nights ago I was awakened by that feeling. You know, the one I get when one of the children are in trouble." She paused. "Only it wasn't one of the children, it was her." Their eyes stared into one another's. The fact that it had been 'that' feeling was significant. Both of them tried to think of an explanation and could not.

Marion continued.

"I got out of bed and came to the kitchen. I went to get a drink and it came again, stronger. It was like a voice told me to look outside. I did, but could not see anything. A storm was raging, fierce, I tell you. Not a light could be seen in the distance." Marion adjusted herself in the seat and went on.

James watched her intently.

"I prayed for help to see what was out there. You would have had to see it with your own eyes, James..." Tears filled Marion's eyes. "The storm parted, like Moses parting the Red Sea, and there out in the churchyard was the girl. I went out there and carried her inside." Marion stated as if it were and everyday occurrence.

"You carried her?" James asked incredulously when Marion finished.

"Yes. From the manger scene to the front room." Marion fiddled with her plate.

"In a blizzard?"

Marion nodded.

"Thank the Lord you didn't kill yourself." James called out, looking up to the heavens. They both laughed.

"After I placed her on the sofa I realized what I had done. Earlier that same day I had to call the neighbor boy to help me take the trash out." They laughed again, and then sobered.

"Sounds to me like you had two miracles." James's voice resonated.

CHAPTER SEVEN
Revelations
December 8th

Samantha awoke to a room filled with dancing rainbows. At first she thought she was dreaming. She raised her hand straight up from the sofa, trying to touch the soft, bright colors.

Maybe she could catch one.

It was morning and the light from the window burst into the room, causing the phenomenon.

It was one of the most beautiful things Samantha had ever seen. None of the chandeliers in her parent's house had ever done this. Maybe it only happened in this house, where love could almost be tasted in the air.

Samantha heard noises in the kitchen.

Within minutes, Marion shuffled into the room, carrying the familiar tray of soup, a glass of water, and medicine.

"Oh, my! I love it when this happens." Marion said as she surveyed the colorful room. Samantha smiled.

"How did you sleep, dear?" Marion asked warmly as she helped Samantha sit and begin to eat.

"Better. I don't really remember yesterday at all." Samantha said, and then sipped the hot soup. It felt good as she swallowed.

"Yesterday was a gloomy day anyway. Today the sun is out again and my husband is home." Marion smiled.

Samantha felt wary as she thought of the old woman's husband. How would he feel about her being here?

Marion saw the worry.

"Don't fret! You'll get to meet him after church. He's already gone for the morning." Marion stood and pointed to the pile of books Marie had brought over. "Those are for you to read, if you like. We don't have a television. I'll be back from church by eleven thirty."

Samantha nodded and kept eating.

Marion left out the front door. Her perfume lingered in the air.

Samantha tried to get up, but couldn't. She was too weak. She noticed her backpack on the floor next to the couch and leaned over to grab it.

It was too heavy.

She lay back down on the couch and drifted back to sleep.

~

When Samantha awakened again there were noises in the kitchen. The deep resonance of a man's voice caught her attention.

Marion's husband!

As Samantha sat up to look over the couch towards the kitchen she saw Marion peek through the doorway.

"You're awake!" Marion said and hurried back into the kitchen. Within minutes she was coming back into the front room with a tall, regal looking man trailing behind.

His eyes were the the most captivating blue Samantha had ever seen.

"Hello, young lady, my name is Reverend James Mahoney. It's a pleasure to meet you." He held out his large hand.

Samantha shook it gingerly, and looked away.

"James and I have been married for forty years." Marion shared as James pulled the two chairs closer to the sofa.

They both sat.

"That's a long time." Was all Samantha could think of to say.

"Marion has filled me in on all she knows of your circumstance and I want you to know that we are both at your service." James said with a quick nod of his head.

This surprised Samantha. What had she expected? Anything but that.

This man was a warm, gentle person, like his wife.

Samantha hadn't known there were people like that. This wasn't what she was used to.

"We will do all we can to help you." James continued. "We only ask for complete honesty. In return we will not contact your family or anyone else without your permission."

Samantha gulped. Tell them everything?

"Is that acceptable to you?" asked James. His eyes seemed to penetrate hers. As if he was looking directly into her.

Samantha thought for a moment.

Marion and James glanced at each other. Before they could adequately help they had to know the truth.

"You promise you won't call my parents?" Samantha asked.

Marion and James both nodded in agreement.

"Okay..." Samantha agreed. "I ran away from home six months ago." Samantha admitted slowly. "I just couldn't let my parents know that I was pregnant."

"Would they have understood?" Marion asked gently.

"No." Samantha stated harshly. "I'm sure my father would have disowned me. It wouldn't have mattered what my Mother thought. She would have supported what ever my father decided. They don't care."

46

There was that statement again. They don't care. Marion knew all too well that there were families out there that didn't know how to love.

"Where do your parents live?" James asked.

"Connecticut. My dad works in New York He's a wall street guy." Samantha said, downplaying the wealth of her family. At the mention of a state so far away both of the Mahoney's eyes widened in surprise.

"How did you ever get out here to Chicago?" Asked Marion in amazement.

"I hitch hiked." Samantha said shrugging her shoulders, as if it were no big deal. She had done what she felt she had to do.

Samantha still wasn't sure why she had chosen Chicago. She just had a feeling that was where she should go. That slightest feeling of some hope in her future gave her the strength to get here.

Once she had gotten to Chicago she wished she hadn't come. But it had taken her a week to get here. She figured she might as well try to make it work.

Marion about fell out of her seat. A sixteen-year-old girl had hitch hiked her way across half the country! It was amazing Samantha had survived!

"You must be an extraordinary young woman to have made it this far." James commented.

Samantha warmed to this man. It was like he understood her. To be understood was something Samantha had always longed for.

"We could call your parents, just to let them know you are all right. I'm sure they are worried." Marion said, hoping that she had not pushed the girl too far.

"No." Samantha said shaking her head. "I don't think they are worrying at all. They are too involved in their social life."

"I won't make you call, but you should know that I think you should." Marion watched Samantha's reaction.

She was dead set against it.

"You think about it. In the meantime, we are going to focus on getting you well." James said, breaking the uncomfortable silence. "Tomorrow Marion will take you to a doctor, to check on the baby."

"What about the baby's father?" Marion asked Samantha.

"He refused to believe it was his. It happened at a party and he said it could have been anyone. But I know it's his." Samantha said with conviction. That confession was hard for her. She hadn't told them about her past. About the problems with her parents and the trouble she frequently got into. She was afraid that they would not help her if they knew. These were good, God fearing people. They would not approve of her anymore that her father had. Though she was beginning to trust them, she was still wary of sharing those types of things. She was sure that even God himself did not approve of her. That thought further dampened her spirits.

"We'll let you rest." James spoke softly. "We can talk more later."

CHAPTER EIGHT
The Time is Coming
December 9th

The next morning Marion took Samantha to an appointment to check the baby.

It was not an easy task.

Samantha was so weak she could hardly walk. With Marion's arm around Samantha's middle they made it from the car to the building, where there was a wheelchair inside the main doors.

Marion helped situate Samantha in the chair, and then they rode the elevator to the third floor.

Samantha's stomach churned at the thought of having to go through this appointment. It was something she had never experienced. She remembered her mother talking about what it was like to have a baby. It had not been easy. Stories of pain and more pain echoed in Samantha's ears, then the memory of her mother saying that it was all worth it, because she got her daughter.

But not for Samantha. She would give her baby up.

The first door down the hallway read, Rachel Humphries, CNM. Samantha asked what the letters meant.

"Certified Nurse Midwife." Marion answered as she opened the door and awkwardly pushed Samantha inside.

~

"Call me Rachel." Said the woman as she entered the examination room.

Rachel had obviously been informed of the situation before hand. She was very tactful and conscious of Samantha's feelings and worries. She explained everything she did as they went along.

The appointment lasted a little over an hour. Samantha had thought it would never end.

Rachel performed a urine test, a blood test, took her blood pressure, weighed her, and asked a lot of questions. Then Samantha was taken into another room where she was told they would do an ultrasound. Samantha didn't know what to expect. Would it hurt?

A screen beside the bed was turned on. Rachel squirted a cold jelly like substance on her stomach then rubbed it around with a device that looked like an electric massager. As she moved it across Samantha's stomach she slowed, then stopped, still holding it against her skin, and pointed up at the screen. Samantha's eyes followed.

She couldn't believe it! There was her baby! Its heart beat quickly and was visible on the screen. Rachel pointed out arms and fingers, then the legs and toes. She pointed out its organs and bones. The baby moved as they watched.

To be able to see inside a body like that! It was amazing!

"Would you like to know what it is?" Rachel asked with a smile.

"No." Samantha refused. She knew that she could not get too attached to this baby. She would want to keep it.

Rachel moved the device around some more, squinting at the screen and making notes on the computer. She explained that she was measuring the baby, to see when the due date would be.

Samantha had felt the child within her, moving around. At times it made her sick, it moved so much.

But what fascinated Samantha more than anything else was the heart. It beat in a steady rhythm that could be seen and heard. Somehow it comforted Samantha.

"You're farther along than I thought. You're so small, it's deceiving."

Both Samantha and Marion waited for Rachel to speak again.

"You should have this baby within the month. I'd better start seeing you once a week."

Samantha's eyes widened. She hadn't realized it would come that fast. Her palms began to sweat. She wasn't ready for this. What would she do? Where would she go?

As Samantha gasped at the revelation, Marion felt relieved.

Marion was aware of a calm reassurance in her heart. This was why she had felt so impressed to help this girl. She wasn't only helping her. She was helping a new life enter this world, and live.

In the car on the way to the Mahoney home, Marion made sure that Samantha knew she was welcome to stay until after she had recovered from having the baby. Marion could see the Samantha was hesitant to accept. She didn't want to take advantage of these nice people.

But she did accept. She had nowhere else to go.

CHAPTER NINE
Sunday Sermon
December 15th

Samantha awoke the following Sunday with a feeling she hadn't felt in months.

She had strength!

Samantha had practically slept the whole week since her appointment with the nurse. She had needed it. Now she felt rejuvenated, ready to tackle life again.

That was another thing she hadn't felt in months.

Since leaving home there had been little to look forward to. Her life had been a matter of survival until the baby came. Then she would be able to go back to her life, her friends, her parents.

No, Samantha thought, she would not go back to her friends. She had learned her lesson. Getting into trouble hadn't gotten her anywhere, but where she was at this moment.

And this was somewhere she would have preferred to have never gotten to.

And her family?

They were something Samantha realized she wasn't sure she wanted. Maybe it would be easier to wash her hands of them and find a new life. Here at the Mahoney's Samantha had tasted of something she had never felt. These people seemed to care for her even though she had made some major mistakes.

The Mahoney's were a breath of fresh air.

Samantha got up off the couch and made her own way into the bathroom, which was something she had needed help with since she had arrived.

The clock in the kitchen read six thirty a.m.

Neither Marion nor James were up yet. Samantha passed the door to their bedroom. It looked as though there was another bedroom at the end of the hall. Marion wondered what was in there.

The Mahoney's house was small, but Samantha found herself more comfortable here than in the three-story, ten thousand square foot house she grew up in. Just seeing how happy the Mahoney's were with so little caused Samantha to question how she had been brought up.

She never remembered not having money and all that wealth brought. As a child she had everything she could have ever wanted. She was happy back then, before she felt that her father didn't love her. But none of the material things had caused her happiness. It had been her state of mind. In fact, she didn't see the material things making her parents happy either. They were always going after things that they didn't have, as if getting the next thing would make them complete.

Back in the living room, Samantha sat on the couch and unzipped her backpack. She hadn't opened it since she'd been here.

Inside were a few of her belongings, a change of clothes, and the book she had taken from her mother.

The book.

During the first month after running away Samantha had forgotten about it. One night when she was missing her mother more than ever before, she had taken it out of her backpack. After opening the front cover it was apparent that it was a journal. The first entry was dated in the 1920's. Samantha had felt a strange pull to the book. She glanced at the entry trying to figure out why it had meant so much to her mother. It didn't make sense. Samantha didn't finish reading. There were more important things to do, like find a job and food.

Samantha picked up the book. As she was about to open the cover, Samantha heard Marion in the kitchen. She put the book back into her backpack and zipped it closed. She would have to look at it later. Right now she was ready for breakfast.

Samantha walked into the kitchen.

Marion stood at the stove, making scrambled eggs, with her back towards Samantha.

"Good morning." Samantha spoke softly.

At the sound of her voice, Marion jerked her head

around in surprise. Her mouth hung open for a moment, and then tightened into a joyful smile.

"Samantha dear! I see you are feeling better!" Marion walked to Samantha and hugged her tightly.

The embrace took Samantha off guard.

Marion guided her to a chair at the table and motioned her to sit down.

"Do you like eggs?" Marion asked as she went back to the stove.

"Yes, they sound good." Samantha answered.

James rushed into the kitchen just as Marion set the plates filled with food on the table.

"Well, good morning!" he greeted as he sat down. James said a quick prayer upon the food, and then they all began to eat.

"If you are feeling well enough, will you come to church with us today?" Marion asked. Samantha looked back and forth between the Mahoney's.

Go to church?

"I haven't been to church since I was a little girl..." Samantha admitted. For a moment there was complete silence.

James could not imagine not going to church. He had always been a church going man. That was why he became a minister. Religion was his whole life. Marion's heart ached at the knowledge this girl did not know God, or the hope that came with religion.

"Good!" James replied. "Come today! It will lift your spirits."

After eating breakfast, Marion found a dress from her closet that Samantha could wear. It wasn't anything Samantha usually would have worn. But it would do.

~

At ten minutes to nine, Marion and Samantha left the house to walk over to the church. People came from every direction, falling into line at the door.

James stood in the doorway shaking hands with people as they passed through. Marion led Samantha around the crowd, explaining that she never waited to shake her husband's hand. Although it would be nice to say hello to him there were plenty of other people that needed to feel of his strength.

Marion chose a bench towards the front on which to sit. Samantha was happy to be able to rest.

Many people greeted Marion as they passed. They would nod or wave to Samantha. Organ music played softly, echoing through the tall room. Large stain-glass windows with flower designs followed the height of the church from behind the podium all the way to the ceiling.

The congregation took their seats as James walked down the center aisle and up to the podium.

"Good morning!" He greeted. "Thank you for coming to worship our Lord and Savior Jesus Christ. He is proud of your effort." James stepped back and sat down as the choir in the seats behind him stood.

They sang a song about Jesus that Samantha had never heard before. Their voices echoed through the room, sounding heavenly. Samantha looked around the room as the choir sang. Here in this building was every type of person that Samantha could imagine. There were families, older couples, and even a few groups of teenagers who sat together towards the back.

When the choir was through James stood up to the podium and a hush fell over the crowd.

"In chapter eleven in the book of John we read of Lazarus." James began. "Now, we know that Jesus was especially close to Lazarus and his two sisters. Yet, when Jesus received word of Lazarus being deathly ill he did not come right away. Why didn't he come right away? Because Lazarus was going to be instrumental in displaying the awesome power of God! Jesus was attending to his Father's plan."

James placed both hands on either side of the podium and looked out into the crowd. His piercing eyes were filled with tears.

Samantha felt a feeling she had not felt before. James went on.

"Then Jesus received word that Lazarus had died. Only then did he go to him. Both sisters of Lazarus asked

Jesus why He had not come to save Lazarus. Why he had let him die! They were angry with Him because they knew Jesus had the power to stay Lazarus's life. Then Jesus said 'I am the resurrection, and the life: he that believeth in me, though he were dead, yet shall he live. And whosoever liveth and believeth in me shall never die.' Those women believed him! They had faith in Jesus!"

Samantha could not take her eyes off James.

"Jesus walked to the tomb where Lazarus lay for the past four days and called him forth." James raised his voice and his eyes to the ceiling. "Jesus raised Lazarus from the dead. He brought him back to life! Why did he do this?" James's voice softened.

Samantha noticed the way everyone looked up at James. They loved him and he loved them.

"He did it for us, so that we may know of His almighty power, that we may know that Jesus is our Savior. He is calling to us to come to Him! We don't need to die to be saved! We can be saved from the mistakes we've made, by becoming His followers. We must forsake our sins and become more like Him! He loves us. He wants us to be happy. He will help us through any obstacle that may be placed in our way. But only if we ask."

Samantha felt warmth flow through her body. She felt the love James spoke of. She longed for that kind of love. Could she really find it here, in a church? In a man named Jesus whom she would never meet?

"Jesus is the way, the truth, and the life. We can repair our lives by accepting his healing grace into our hearts. He can live within our hearts, if we will just let him in." James's gaze fell on Samantha. It was if her were talking directly to her. "Look to Jesus for strength. He is there, waiting for you."

James's words had left such a great impact on Samantha that she hardly remembered getting home.

Marion noticed how quiet Samantha was. She sensed the wheels in Samantha's head were turning. Marion prayed that Samantha would believe. Jesus could give her more strength than anything else, anywhere.

That night, as Samantha lay in bed she thought of the sermon. Something in her stirred again at the thought of Jesus caring for her! Was it possible?

CHAPTER TEN
Coming Clean
December 16th

"Can Jesus help someone like me?" Samantha asked Marion the next morning after James had left to attend to church duties. This thought had been on her mind since yesterday during the sermon James had given. Samantha had gone to church as a child, but she never had comprehended that Jesus could actually help a person through their difficulties. Now, that very question was at the front of Samantha's mind.

Marion looked up at Samantha, knowing that her prayer yesterday had been heard. Samantha's heart had been opened and she was ready to hear about Jesus.

"Yes. He can." Marion sat in the chair next to Samantha at the table. For a moment there was silence, then Marion spoke.

"There was a time in my life that I thought God could never love me, not after the sins I had committed." Marion admitted.

Samantha looked up at Marion in surprise. It had never crossed her mind that this perfectly faithful woman would have ever felt that way. Marion seemed like the type of person that had always been perfect.

"You?" Samantha asked.

"Yes, believe it or not, I have not always been old and wise." Marion said. "I grew up going to church with my parents. Every Sunday that I can remember, I and my three brothers sat on the front row in the church down the street from our house." Marion smiled as she remembered. "Then my granny died. Her death made me angry with God. I needed my granny. She was the only one who really knew me. I turned away from God at the time I needed Him the most and it took a whole lot to bring me back around. I did a lot of things that I shouldn't have because I was angry at the world." Marion said, opening up her heart.

"Really?" Samantha asked trying to believe that she too could become like Marion. Maybe there was hope for her.

Samantha wondered what it was that Marion had done. But, she didn't dare ask. "What brought you back?" Samantha asked instead.

Marion waited a few moments before answering. She looked off into the distance seeing things that only she could see.

"A little girl..." Marion's voice trailed off. Her eyes filled with tears and she looked down at the table. She brought her wrinkled arms against her chest, almost hugging herself. "Sometimes tragic things happen in our lives and they are the only things that make us see what's really important."

Marion felt the usual throw of emotions encompass her as she allowed her mind to wander through the past she kept so tightly locked away.

"But it wasn't just her. It only started with her. I met James and he turned my life around." Tears began to fall from Marion's eyes, sliding down her cheeks.

Samantha thought of the last six months. She wished she could take it all back. She wished that she had never gotten pregnant, that she hadn't run away. But even as she wished it she knew that things still would have been hard at home. The problem with her father ran deep.

Tears began to fall from Samantha's eyes too.

Marion grabbed Samantha and pulled her to her in an embrace. She knew the pain the girl felt. She knew what it was like to forsake everything, to give up your life, to give up on yourself. Marion wanted to do all she could for this girl so she wouldn't end up like Marion had, with no family.

There was more to life than protecting your pride, which was what Marion had done all those years ago. There was more to life than living up to everyone's expectations. The relationship between yourself and God was the most important. Everyone made mistakes, but how we deal with those mistakes is what will form the path of the rest of our lives. Out of all the trials Marion had experienced she had learned one unifying principle. Be true to yourself, be true to God. If that is accomplished then all else will fall into place. It had taken a lifetime of living with the consequences of her choices for Marion to come to that realization. She wished she would have known that earlier in her life, perhaps she wouldn't have tried to kill herself instead of face the consequences.

Marion replayed the scene in her mind.

It was night and the river was moving rapidly because of the storm. She had stood on the bridge, getting ready to jump.

All she could think about was how her parents had told her to leave. She was a bad example to the younger children. She wasn't worthy of being part of their family.

Marion jumped into the churning water below.

But she didn't die. Someone had seen her. A man had jumped in after her and pulled her out, unconscious but breathing.

At the hospital the doctor confirmed what Marion had already known. Not only had that man saved her, but the unborn child she was carrying.

Marion left the hospital alone. She did not go back home.

Samantha watched as Marion saw the awful events in her mind. The old woman's shoulders seemed to sag even more than usual as she cried. Instinctively Samantha knew what Marion had gone through.

"You had a baby, didn't you? A baby before you were married, just like me."

"Yes, and I gave it up as you are planning to do." Marion confirmed as she wiped the tears away from the wrinkles around her eyes.

"Do you regret it?" Samantha asked, wanting to know.

"I don't regret giving her to a family who would love her. I do regret that I was never able to reconcile with my parents. I've spent my whole life without them."

Marion looked up into Samantha's tearful eyes.

"Samantha, don't let this tear you away from your parents. This could be something to help you become closer to them. Contacting them won't be easy. It might take years to overcome the differences. But at least you would have your family." Marion pleaded with Samantha.

Samantha's heart went out to Marion. A bond fused between the two of them. They had something in common, something that neither of them had resolved. But, Samantha had the chance to resolve it.

"I'll think about it..." Samantha said, realizing that what Marion had said made sense. How could her parents ever understand her if she didn't let them get to know her?

Not all the blame rested upon her father's shoulders. Yes, he had fault. But, their relationship was something that could be worked on.

Samantha realized she had pushed her parents away.

Going home after having the baby would not change anything. They would want to know why she had left and where she had been. By not answering their questions the gap would only widen. What had she done? Despite the problems she wanted to see her parents again. She didn't want them to banish her because of this.

Samantha knew what she had to do. She had to tell the truth. She couldn't hide any longer. She would face it head on and pray that God would help her father understand.

"I'll call them." Samantha said. Marion grabbed her again, hugging her even tighter. More tears fell from her eyes. But this time they were tears of joy. Marion was sure that Samantha was doing the right thing.

"I'll help you. I'll be here for you." Marion crooned.

They cried together, and talked some more. By the end of the day, despite the great age difference, a deep friendship had begun. They found that they both liked to draw. Marion had taken art classes in school, just as Samantha had. Marion told Samantha of the disapproval of her parents. Samantha understood the pain it caused and began to share the problems she and her father had.

Marion told Samantha of the night she had found her out in the snow. How she had been given a miracle. Samantha marveled at what had happened. She had never seen a miracle take place, now one had happened to her. Everything seemed so unreal, yet at the same time, nothing had made this much sense ever before.

There was a part of Samantha's heart that began to believe that God really was there for her. She just hadn't known how to listen or ask for help.

The feeling that resulted between them was the belief that they must have known each other in heaven. Samantha had been sent to Marion for help because she was the person placed in the right place at the right time to help.

Samantha would call home tomorrow night.

CHAPTER ELEVEN
Calling Home
December 17th

Samantha awoke from a restless sleep at five a.m. Her night had been filled with dreams of calling home. Good dreams, bad dreams. In one dream she called home and found that the number had been disconnected. In another she had called home and a girl answered. Someone had come and taken her place and her father was happy. In yet another dream her father just hung up on her.

That's what she was afraid of, afraid that her parents would not want to talk to her. What if they had taken steps to avoid any further communication?

No. Samantha couldn't think of that.

They did have love for her. She had always felt it from her mother. Her Father's version of love was warped and mangled. But it was the only love he knew how to give.

Despite all that had happened it had been Samantha's decision to leave. They had not forced her. Perhaps there was a chance for reconciliation.

Samantha knew that she could not call during the day. Her parents were busy people. If she called after four in the afternoon her mother would be home. That was who Samantha wanted to talk to first. After the initial shock of finally hearing from her only daughter, her mother might understand.

Maybe her mother could soften her father's reaction.

~

Samantha was quiet during breakfast.

Both James and Marion were well aware of the thoughts that were forming in the young girl's mind. She was scared of what would happen when she called home. They wanted to comfort her, to tell her that everything would be all right.

But they couldn't. They didn't know what the outcome would be.

"Samantha, I have faith that whatever happens will be God's will. Trust in Him, pray to Him. He will help you." James said with conviction as he left for the day.

Samantha decided to do just that. But, she wasn't sure how to pray.

~

"Marion?" Samantha approached hesitantly after breakfast had been cleaned up.

"Yes, dear?" Marion responded.

"I want to be ready for this afternoon when I call my parents. And I feel like I should pray." Samantha stumbled over her words. "Can you tell me how to pray?"

"Of course!" Marion's smile warmed Samantha's heart. They went to the living room and knelt next to the sofa. It took a moment for Marion to get down on her knees.

"We always open a prayer by greeting God. There are many ways to greet him. It's up to you to decide how you'll do it. Then we thank Him for the things we have. Only when we are through thanking him do we ask for his help and blessings. Then we close the prayer in His name and say 'Amen'." Samantha took it all in, trying her hardest to remember the order it was to be done. Marion could see how hard she was trying to catalog it all.

"Let me say one, then you can." Marion said. They lowered their heads towards their clasped hands and Marion said a simple, yet genuine prayer. When she finished she looked at Samantha.

"Okay." Samantha stated. "I can do it, I think." Again they lowered their heads and this time Samantha prayed. She stumbled over her words, but she managed to say a prayer that brought tears to both of their eyes. Never before had Samantha felt so close to God. It was as if she knew he was there and that she was doing the right thing in talking to him.

"That was a wonderful prayer, Samantha. Just remember to say what is in your heart. That's what God wants to hear."

~

Through the day, as Marion cleaned her house, she kept an eye on Samantha. The girl had found a Bible on the shelf in the front room and was curled up on the couch reading it.

At four o'clock, Marion went to the front room to see if Samantha was ready. She found Samantha on her knees, praying. Large tears dripped down her cheeks. Samantha made no attempt to wipe them away as she silently prayed.

Marion waited, her own eyes filling with tears as well. She herself had carried a prayer in her heart all day, willing and wanting the outcome to be good.

Samantha lifted her eyes and met Marion's stare. Without speaking Samantha went to the kitchen, picked up the phone and dialed.

Samantha's heart beat faster and faster with every ring. Her palms started sweating. She desperately wanted to hang up the phone and run, run far away.

But she knew she couldn't do that. Running hadn't solved anything.

A voice on the other end of the line picked up.

"Hello, Stately residence." Said a woman with a heavy Spanish accent. Samantha did not recognize the voice.

"I'd like to speak with Lorna Stately please." Samantha said with a shaky voice.

"May I tell her who's calling?"

"Just tell her it's very important." Samantha responded.

"Yes, mame." The woman said curtly and put Samantha on hold. Samantha waited. The silence almost too much for her to take.

Then, her mother was there.

"Hello?" Lorna asked. She sounded hurried.

Samantha froze with fear. Marion noticed the reaction and placed a firm hand on Samantha's shoulder. She was here for moral support.

"Hello, Mother." Samantha said, ready to cry. It had been so long since she had heard her mother's voice.

"Samantha?" Lorna asked shocked at what she was hearing. "Samantha is that really you?"

"Yes. Mother it's me. I wanted to let you know that I'm alright." Samantha began. A harsh noise on the other end stopped Samantha. Then her father's voice filled her ears.

"Where have you been?" Charles demanded, not an ounce of concern evident in his voice.

"I ran away." Samantha admitted. She held her breath and waited for the tirade.

It came, just as expected.

"Well of course you ran away! After all I've given you, that's how you repay me? You run away and leave no word for half a year? Do you have any idea what you've put your mother through?" He didn't wait for an explanation, just kept on. "Samantha your behavior over the last three years has been unacceptable. Do you hear me? Unacceptable!"

"I wanted to tell you why I left." Samantha blurted out.

"Then tell me!" Charles barked.

Samantha took a deep breath and looked to Marion for support.

"I'm pregnant. I was afraid to tell you."

There was silence as Charles grasped at what his daughter had said. Samantha held her breath. She could hear his breathing intensify. His anger grew and grew until he could not contain it.

"Don't you ever come back to this house! You've disgraced this family for the last time!" Charles yelled into the phone.

The line went dead.

Samantha pulled the phone away from her ear. She could not hold the tears back. They streamed down her face, thick and heavy.

Marion wrapped her arms around the girl. She had heard the last words the man had yelled.

It was like a knife into Marion's heart as well. Her father had said the same thing.

Years of hurt boiled to the surface. Samantha yanked herself away from Marion and slapped her hands against the table in anger.

"He's treated me like nothing for my entire life! What did he think I would do? I would've done almost anything to make him proud of me! And yet nothing ever worked!

So I stopped trying. I started doing things to make him mad. Things that I knew would hurt him! And even though mother cared, she was too afraid of making him mad to help me! I hate him! I hate him!" Samantha collapsed to the floor, crying so hard that she could not breathe.

Marion let Samantha cry, then when the crying slowed; she helped the girl into the front room.

"You should rest. It's been a rough day. We'll talk about it tomorrow, alright?" Marion's brow furrowed. Samantha had become almost unresponsive. Had calling the girl's parents been the right thing?

Yes. Marion felt it with all her heart. It had been the right thing.

Samantha would heal; she would do all she could to become the great person she was meant to be, even if her family would never accept her.

After all, that's what Marion had done.

CHAPTER TWELVE
A Firm Decision
Bedtime

Samantha was heartbroken over the words her father had spoken. He spoke them out of anger, she was aware of that. But, it didn't make them hurt any less. In times past Samantha had been able to brush it all away. She used to drink. She never felt better than when she had been drinking.

But, there would be no drinking tonight.

Samantha had given it up when she found out she was pregnant. Since then, life seemed to be one long line of struggles that she could not ever escape from.

And now this.

There had been far too many times that her father had said things that hurt. Countless arguments broke out between them and most of them ended up in irreparable damage.

But this time the pain was almost unbearable.

This time Samantha was sure she would never see her family ever again. Tonight she had become an orphan.

What had she expected? Had she really thought that by leaving and not telling them where she had gone things would be better?

Yes. She had thought that. Had she been wrong? Would it have been better to have stayed and faced the situation head on? Samantha wasn't sure.

What if she had never met Marion? Samantha couldn't imagine life without the Mahoney's. Why was that? Why had she let herself create such a bond with two people she hardly knew?

That wasn't true.

Samantha felt like she knew Marion. Even Marion had agreed that they must've been friends in heaven. Could all this be fate? Was this the way things were supposed to happen?

Samantha couldn't believe that God would rip apart her natural family. What purpose was there in that?

She shook her head and lay down on the couch.

What was she thinking? God didn't have time to plan out little things like this. He had better things to do.

But, thinking that God did have a hand in it brought comfort to Samantha.

A loud growl erupted from her stomach.

She had been so distraught she had skipped dinner. Samantha rose from the couch and walked to the kitchen. There would be something she could eat.

Marion sat at the kitchen table, her head down, her arms folded against her. Samantha stopped at the door and waited for her to finish praying. When Marion's head lifted, Samantha ventured into the room.

"Is there anything I can eat?" Samantha asked quietly. She didn't want to be a bother.

Marion smiled warmly, happy to see Samantha up and hungry.

"I saved you a plate. It's in the fridge. I'll warm it up for you." Marion rose from her chair and retrieved the food. While it warmed Marion addressed Samantha.

"How are you doing?" Marion knew it was a loaded question, but she couldn't think of any other way to ask it.

"Okay, I guess. It's weird, every time I've felt this bad in the past nothing would help. It's different this time. I mean I feel awful. But at the same time I feel a little bit of peace. I can't help but think that the only thing that's made the difference tonight is what you've told me about God." Samantha shrugged her shoulders.

Marion smiled.

"When my father told me I could never return to his house, I felt the same way. My faith and belief in God was the only thing that pulled me through. Without those spiritual feelings I would never have decided to give up my child. But it was the best thing." Marion paused for a moment, then asked a question that had been on her mind. "What caused you to believe that you should give up your baby?"

Samantha thought for a moment before answering. She had never really thought about it. She never questioned what she would do with the baby. Adoption had always been the only answer in her mind.

Then it became clear to her.

"My mother was adopted." Samantha said, recalling the stories her mother had told her. "Even though she always wanted to meet her real mother, she loved her adopted family. She wouldn't have traded them for anything."

Marion's heart swelled. Hearing about someone who had been adopted and had a good experience reaffirmed that she had made the right decision to give up her child. Wherever she was, Marion was sure that her little girl had a good life.

Only she wouldn't be a little girl anymore. She would have a family of her own. As Marion thought of what she might be like she realized she would give anything to peek in on the life of her daughter, the life she had missed. But, it didn't matter what an old woman wished. Life had a way of going on without you.

"Marion?" Samantha questioned. Marion looked like she was a million miles away.

"Yes, sorry." Marion pulled herself back into reality. "I'm glad you've chosen adoption, Samantha. It's the best choice in your circumstance."

"I know. I guess if this baby is coming soon I'd better get the ball rolling."

Marion and Samantha looked at each other, knowing full well that this process wouldn't be easy.

"I'll call a friend of mine who works with adoptions in the morning. I've known her for years." Marion stated. She lifted her old hazel eyes to meet Samantha's. "You're sure, dear?"

"Yes." Was all Samantha said, but it was all that was needed.

CHAPTER THIRTEEN
Going into Town
December 18th

The next morning, like she said she would, Marion called Tracey Aviat. Tracey worked in an adoption center in Chicago. They had known each other for years, through church. Marion had been involved in many adoption cases, so this was nothing new to her.

"Bring Samantha in and we'll fill out the paperwork." Tracey relayed.

Marion hung up the phone. Samantha watched her from across the table, expectantly.

"We'll take you into town and fill out papers whenever you're ready. Then everything will be settled." Marion said. "The office is in Chicago. We could make a day of it. Chicago is beautiful during Christmas time. But, only if you're willing to slow down and help an old woman around town. I don't have as much umph as I used to."

"Can we go today?" Samantha asked wanting to get it over with.

"We probably can, if you're up to it." Marion said, looking Samantha up and down. "You look pretty tired." Marion herself felt tired. Her age was catching up to her. Not many sixty year old women could keep up with her but she certainly wasn't a spring chicken.

"I'm up for it." Samantha assured her. Nothing could keep her from taking this step.

~

Marion called James, to let him know where they were going and before they knew it they were off.

"I don't usually take the car into town, but today is an exception. Parking is expensive compared to paying the price of a ticket for the train." Marion said as she pulled the dark green Buick out of the driveway. They waved to James who was outside the church talking with a man dressed in a suit.

The drive to downtown Chicago went quickly. Marion and Samantha rode in silence, both of their minds running in high gear. There were so many things to think about.

There were so many decisions in life, Marion thought to herself. At Samantha's age she had no idea where life would take her.

They traveled south, down Lake Shore Drive. The lake gleamed against the sun on one side of the road, while skyscrapers stood high on the other.

"I love this road." Marion broke the silence. "The scenery is beautiful. On a clear day you can almost see Michigan from the top of the John Hancock."

As they drove into town, Marion pointed out 'the water tower', an old chapel-like building. As they crossed the Chicago River, Marion pointed at it.

"It's so green. Did you know they had to reverse the flow of that thing?" Samantha only nodded. There was too much on her mind.

Downtown Chicago was beautiful. Decorations hung on every lamp post and lights were wrapped around every tree. At night the lights would be beautiful. But they wouldn't be staying long enough to see them. Marion drove Samantha down Michigan Ave. telling her of fond memories she had here as a child.

"There's an outdoor ice skating rink right over there." Marion pointed across the way.

"I used to skate at the outdoor rink in New York when I was little." Samantha shared. She had some good memories there, memories where she and her father had played together, laughing and chasing one another.

But to Samantha Chicago represented her desolation, here, right off this very road they were on was where Samantha had suffered more than anywhere else. Chicago was something she did not want to remember.

Samantha wanted to ask Marion to stop talking. She just wanted to be alone with her thoughts. But she knew the old woman was only trying to help. So, instead of ruining the fun for Marion, Samantha put on a happy face and listened to the stories, trying to imagine them.

Tracey Aviat was a kind woman who understood the pain associated with giving up a child. She was considerate of Samantha and allowed her plenty of time to go through each step of the process. They filled out the necessary paperwork. Then Samantha searched the books of prospective parents. She hadn't know that she would be able to pick out the family her baby would go to, or even that she would be sent information on how the baby was doing for the first five years of it's life. Samantha felt better knowing that she would be aware of what was happening. She felt more and more secure of her decision to give her baby up for adoption.

But picking the parents was hard. There were so many good choices. They all looked so nice.

"Marion, how do I choose?" Samantha asked.

"Maybe you should let God choose." Marion stated simply. Samantha thought about it.

"How do I know who God chooses?" Samantha looked up from the book at Marion.

"Pray to Him about each couple you are considering, then listen to your feelings. When God answers prayers we feel a warm fuzzy feeling inside. So, wait for that feeling, when it comes you will know that you and God are on the same page." Marion made the process of prayer sound so simple. Samantha wasn't sure she could do it. But she was willing to give it a try.

"Thank you Marion." Samantha took a deep breath. "I guess I need some time alone." Marion gave Samantha a hug before leaving. She closed the door behind her and sat in the lobby.

Once she was alone, Samantha made a list of her top choices of parents. Then, she got down on her knees and prayed about each one of them. At the eleventh set of names she was beginning to think that she didn't know how to get an answer. She prayed again. Nothing.

She prayed again, about the next set of names. A warm feeling filled her heart and Samantha felt like jumping for joy. She had found them! These were the people who would be the parents of her child!

~

During the drive back to Evanston Samantha related her experience in getting an answer to her prayer. Though it seemed familiar to Marion, it was completely new to Samantha. Now, more than ever, Samantha believed that God did have a personal interest in her. He was there for her and He would help her get though this.

Marion could not keep her mind from traveling backwards to the day she had signed away her daughter's life to someone else. It had been the hardest thing she had ever done.

She wasn't allowed to have any contact with the family.

The caseworker had told Marion only one thing. The new parents were unable to have any children of their own and desperately wanted a girl.

Her little girl would have a good home. She was happy that Samantha would be able to get news of her child.

At dinner James and Marion told Samantha about the Christmas party to be held on Saturday.

"Would you be up to helping me get things ready?" Marion asked excitedly. "Our back bedroom is full of half finished decorations and table settings."

"Sure. It sounds like fun!" Samantha replied feeling surprised that she was looking forward to a little Christmas fun.

"Good! We'll start tomorrow morning!" Marion and James grasped each other's hands and smiled at Samantha.

CHAPTER FOURTEEN
The Christmas Party
December 21st

Saturday came quickly.

Marion had kept Samantha busy Thursday and Friday helping prepare for the Christmas Party to be held Saturday night. Together, they spent the morning hours in the building next to the chapel, decorating, with the help of a few others. Other people were building the set for the Nativity play held every year.

Samantha watched as members of the congregation rehearse the play on the other side of the room.

This was nothing like Samantha thought it would be. There wasn't hired help doing all the work. These were the people who would attend, all working their hardest to make the evening a success.

When the preparations were finished, Marion and Samantha walked back home to get ready. They showered and dressed for the evening.

~

At six o'clock sharp the party began.

The three of them arrived together, James, Marion, and Samantha. James quickly took his place at the doorway to shake hands. Marion had to check on the food.

Instead of tagging along, Samantha chose a table towards the back and sat down on a chair, feeling completely exhausted. It had been a long day.

She watched as crowds of people entered the room. James shook the hand of every person as they entered. Many people were dressed in t-shirts and sweatshirts that bore Christmas symbols.

The adults lingered at the door talking to friends and neighbors while the children raced towards Santa, laughing and talking about what they were going to ask for.

Samantha recalled the first time she met Santa. It was at Bloomingdale's while she was Christmas shopping with her mother. It had been a wonderful day. Though Samantha was only five she remembered it vividly. The store was filled with Christmas. Red bows, green garland, gold and silver bulbs decorated Christmas trees that lit every corner of the store.

Tonight Santa sat in a large velvet chair in one corner of the room. A large Christmas tree covered with home-made ornaments towered next to him. A narrow red carpet led the way to his chair, signaling that Santa was the guest of honor. He wore the usual red coat with white fur trim, red pants, and black boots. A large white beard hung from his face, accentuating his overly rosy cheeks.

On either side of him stood an elf. As each child climbed off Santa's lap, they were given a large red and white candy cane with a green ribbon tied around it.

In another corner stood an old piano. The wood was worn, scratched all over from the many parties it had been played at. An elderly woman sat at it, playing an assortment of familiar Christmas carols that could be heard through out the large room. Couples had gathered around to dance to the music.

On the far wall was the Nativity set on a small stage. Chairs were lined up in rows facing it, empty and waiting until the play began.

Dinner was being served from a table along the wall. Starting off the line were piles of paper plates and plastic utensils. Four large turkeys sat in a row. Servers carved off generous slices. Then came the mashed potatoes, steamy vegetables, a couple green salads and a large variety of Jell-O salads. The dessert table was filled with different cakes, brownies, cookies, and homemade candies.

This party was nothing compared to the parties her parents would throw. No one dressed in formal attire. There was no orchestra playing. The food was not nearly so ornate or abundant. But, Samantha felt how much the people were enjoying themselves and realized that it was as good a party as she had ever been to

Marion returned and pulled Samantha over to get a plate of food. While they were in line, Marion introduced Samantha to the people around them. It amazed Samantha how many people Marion knew! She must have known every person at the party!

James joined them at a table as they ate. His eyes were bright with enjoyment. To him, it was heaven on earth to see his congregation having fun.

It was Christmas! It was time to celebrate!

At quarter to seven a plump woman wearing a red and green plaid dress tapped Marion on the shoulder and whispered something in her ear. They both looked at Samantha, and then went back to whispering. The woman left as quickly as she had come.

Samantha watched the woman rush away, wondering where she had ever found a dress like that. She returned her attention to Marion.

Samantha cocked her head to one side, wanting Marion to tell her what their secret had been about. Uneasiness spread through her.

"Mrs. Raymore is directing the re-enactment this year. I guess their Mary has the stomach flu." Marion said sadly. "She wasn't sure what to do until she looked over here, at us."

Samantha wasn't sure what Marion meant.

James eyed Marion closely, and then realized what had happened. They both looked at Samantha, their eyes sparkling.

"Samantha, I think you've been nominated to play the part of Mary." James revealed.

CHAPTER FIFTEEN
Mary, Mother of Jesus
Moments Later...

She couldn't be Mary!

"I can't do that!" Samantha protested loudly.

"You're the closest thing to a Mary that we have." Marion said as she pulled Samantha to her feet and gently shoved her towards the waiting woman.

"You'll do wonderfully." Samantha heard James call as she made her way to the wings of the stage where she would receive instructions.

~

As Samantha walked on the stage with Joseph, the crowd hushed. With a light blue sheet wrapped around her and a piece of white material draped over her long dark hair, she looked the part. No one could take their eyes off her.

Samantha shook from nervousness. She didn't know what to do! Joseph, put his arm around her and guided her in the right direction.

Together, as the narrator read from scripture, they walked towards an inn, were turned away, and walked to the next.

When they settled into the stable, it was as if it all became real.

Samantha became Mary.

She felt the baby kicking inside her. She felt the sense of urgency.

The baby was coming! Baby Jesus was coming!

As they sat in the hay, Samantha realized that she and Mary had something in common. For that moment it was as if all her mistakes melted away. She envisioned herself as Mary.

She knew how Mary would have felt, traveling around, looking for a place to have her child when there was none. Needing and asking for help when no one would help them.

Mary bore the Son of God! There were no doctors to assist, or a nice clean hospital. There was just Mary, Joseph, and a loving God watching from heaven above.

At the time of the birth of Jesus the room went dark.

In the darkness Samantha was handed a warm squirming bundle. She held it tightly, afraid that she would drop it.

The lights came up and Samantha looked down into the blue eyes of a baby. The child smiled at her and reached a tiny hand up to her face.

That was when the tears started to fall.

Samantha would have this baby alone. Her mother would not be there, nor would her father, or the father of the child. She would not be able to hold the baby close to her and think of how life would be with a new addition, someone new to love with all her heart.

No. Instead a couple would be waiting with excitement. Waiting for their baby, the one they had wanted and never been able to have.

Samantha had found God because of her mistakes. The couple who had experienced so much heartache over not having a child would finally receive their fondest desire. And Samantha was the reason their dream would come true.

Sometimes out of the darkest of situations the most beloved dreams are revealed and given to us.

Jesus was born in the most humble of circumstances and became perfect and saved the world!

Samantha was sure that Jesus could bless her baby with a good home. She had faith in Him.

Samantha realized that there was no better gift she could give those people or the child she would bear than a loving family who would cherish, protect, and give all the love the child would ever need.

Applause interrupted Samantha's thoughts. She had been completely lost in her mind and had missed the end of the show.

She raised her eyes to the audience and saw the tears in many eyes, just like in her own.

Samantha caught sight of Marion. She was crying too.

Before Samantha could realize it someone had taken the baby from her and people were all around her congratulating her on her performance.

Pride swelled in Samantha's heart. She had accomplished something wonderful. Her image had sparked the feelings of Christmas in the hearts of all these people.

Marion threw her arms around Samantha.

"You were wonderful. You look just like her!" Marion whispered in her ear.

"I felt just like her." Samantha whispered back.

CHAPTER SIXTEEN
Early Morning Pains
December 22nd

It was four thirty in the morning when Samantha was awakened by a sharp pain across her stomach.

As it subsided, Samantha took in a deep breath and exhaled slowly. She had never felt a cramp like that. She sat up hoping movement would help the muscles. But, now the pain was gone.

Samantha lay back down and closed her eyes, wanting to return to the dream she had been having.

It was of her mother, holding the book Samantha had taken from off her dresser. She was pleading for it to be read. Samantha's outstretched hand had been ready to take it when she had awakened.

Samantha willed her mind to return to the dream. Just as she fell asleep the pain came again!

Again Samantha held her breath and waited for the pain to subside. It did. She took another deep breath, willing her body to relax.

After four more similar pains, a thought crossed Samantha's mind.

Was the baby coming?

Samantha's heart started to race. She wasn't ready! This couldn't be happening, not yet!

She sat up and swung her legs off the couch, sitting in an upright position and squinted to see the face of the grandfather clock. Five-thirty.

It had been an hour since the first pain had come.

Should she go get Marion? Samantha gauged the time she would have until the next pain. If she went now she should get there before another one came.

Just as Samantha stood, another pain hit. This time it was worse and had come faster than she thought it would.

Samantha let out a gasp and almost fell to the floor. She braced herself against the couch. How would she get to Marion? Tears began to fall from her eyes.

~

Marion blinked her eyes open.

It was dark. She squeezed them shut, wanting to go back to sleep. But couldn't. A persistent, nagging feeling, tugged at her.

There it was again. That feeling. Marion sat up in bed.

"Marion, what is it?" James asked in a sleepy voice.

"I don't know. Something's not right...." Marion's voice trailed off into the darkness.

"Samantha!" Marion called out. "It's Samantha." She climbed out of bed, forgetting about her bathrobe, and raced to the front room. James followed closely behind.

~

In the front room, Samantha was kneeling against the sofa; hands pressed together, knuckles white. She was breathing quick, heavy breaths.

Marion instantly knew what was happening.

Samantha was in labor.

"Breathe easy, slow... slower..." Marion directed as she placed her old hands on Samantha's shoulders.

Samantha listened to Marion's voice as she guided her through yet another contraction. When it subsided, Samantha looked up at Marion and James. Their eyes were filled with concern.

"How did you know?" Samantha asked Marion wearily.

"Just one of those feelings." Marion shrugged. Samantha wasn't fooled with Marion's casualness.

Marion had felt what was happening and again she had come to her rescue.

"How long have you been having contractions?" Marion asked.

"About an hour and a half. Maybe a little more." Samantha tightened as another one came. Marion again coached her through.

"I'm going to call the doctor and let her know we are on our way to the hospital." James said and retreated to the kitchen.

"I'll go get dressed and be right back to help you." Marion said and rushed out of the room, leaving Samantha alone.

Another pain came and Samantha thought of her mother. She wanted to call her. She wanted her to be here! But she couldn't, not after what happened when she had called home.

The dream Samantha had of her mother came to her mind.

For some reason, Samantha felt the dream meant something. Her mother had been trying to give her the book. She had wanted her to read it. Why? What was inside that book that was so significant? She had to find out.

Samantha bent to retrieve the book from her backpack when a strange wetness suddenly flowed from her body.

"There's water! Water!" Samantha called out, hoping that Marion could hear her.

She did.

Within minutes they were headed out to the car. James supported Samantha's weight. Marion carried the bag that had been packed with clothes and things Marion had bought for Samantha to take to the hospital. After giving James a big hug, Marion took the driver's seat.

"I'll be there soon." Said James just before they drove off. He had let Marion know that he would not be coming with them. There was something he felt like he had to do first.

CHAPTER SEVENTEEN
A Prompting
A Little Later...

James watched Marion and Samantha drive away. He should have gone with them, but felt there was something he had to do before following.

It was a cold night. No stars could be seen in the sky. It smelled like snow.

His mind wandered to the girl.

Samantha...

There was something about Samantha. He couldn't put his finger on it. He had felt it since the moment he met her. Marion felt it too. Neither of them had made any sense of it. At times there was such a sense of familiarity, yet they were sure they had never met her before the night Marion had found her.

And Marion's reaction to the girl... She might as well have stated she was going adopt her, make her one of her own. Marion had never attached herself to a stranger like this before.

But Samantha had never felt like a stranger. There was a kinship between her and Marion. James felt it. But there was something else. Something he could not figure out.

What was it?

James silently prayed to God, asking for some kind of help at placing together the pieces he felt in his heart, the pieces that didn't seem to make sense.

A warm feeling flowed through his body as his mind filled with thoughts. He knew what he needed to do.

He walked with determination to the front room.

There on the floor, beside the sofa, was the backpack Samantha had brought with her. He sat on the couch and placed the backpack on his lap. With strong hands he pulled the zipper back, revealing the contents. He pulled them out one at a time and placed them on the sofa next to him. He would know what he was looking for when he found it.

There was a pair of jeans, a t-shirt, a notebook, a pen, a wallet, a zip-lock baggie filled with cough lozenges, a scruffy teddy bear, and an old book.

Odd that the girl would have such an old book in her possession. It was well worn, as if it had been read many times before.

As he opened the front cover, a small piece of paper fell out. On it was the name of Samantha's parents, their home address, and a telephone number.

Again the warm feeling spread through his body. Yes, he knew what he needed to do.

James took the paper to the telephone and dialed.

It rang, and rang, and rang again. Then was answered by a sleepy voice, a woman's voice. "Hello..."

"This is Reverend James Mahoney. I need to speak with Mrs. Lorna Stately." He stated calmly, but could not hide the undertone of urgency.

"This is she." Said the voice, suddenly sounding completely awake.

"Mrs. Stately. Your daughter had been staying with us. I thought you would want to know that she has gone into labor and is at the hospital."

There was silence.

"Mrs. Stately, your daughter needs you..."

CHAPTER EIGHTEEN
At the Hospital
An Hour Later...

When James arrived at the hospital he was directed to the Maternity Ward, which was located on the fourth floor. He walked slowly, thinking of the conversation he had with Samantha's mother just an hour before.

He had told her that Samantha needed her. He wasn't sure she would come. He prayed she would. Samantha needed her mother more than anything else.

He found Samantha settled into a labor and delivery room. Her contractions were three minutes apart, barely giving her enough time to rest in between. They were getting harder and harder for her to bear.

Marion sat at her side, like a steady pillar of strength. James had never seen Marion so dedicated, not quite like this.

"James!" Marion greeted, not leaving Samantha's side. "I'm so glad you're here! The nurse says her progress is slow. We'll just have to wait."

Another pain hit and Samantha called out. Marion grasped Samantha's hands, allowing Samantha to squeeze as hard as she could. Samantha's knuckles turned white.

When it was over Samantha lay back against the firm pillow and closed her eyes. She was tired and wished the baby would just come. She wasn't afraid of the pain. She just wanted to get it over with.

The hospital had admitted her, without insurance, but had informed her that she would not have the luxuries afforded to most patients. That meant no epidural. She would have to have her baby the old fashioned way. This scared Samantha. She wasn't sure what to expect. She only knew that having a baby was painful. She said a silent prayer that she would be able to bear it all.

~

Three hours had passed with little progress. Samantha's body hadn't fully recovered from the months of not eating. It had only been three weeks since she had began recuperating. She wasn't sure she had the strength to continue.

"I can't do it, Marion. I just can't." Samantha puffed between contractions.

"Yes, you can. And you will." Marion said firmly, hoping to give Samantha the strength to go on.

Almost before Samantha had enough time to take another breath she was hit again with the strongest pain she had experienced yet.

At Samantha's yell of pain, Marion signaled for the nurse. The nurse entered the room, took one look at Samantha and called for the doctor.

"The baby's head is crowning." The nurse said as she hurried out of the room. Moments later a staff of people, including Rachel, entered the room and prepared for the birth.

"Hello, Samantha," said Rachel. "I need you to help me all right?" Samantha nodded. "When I tell you to push I need you to use all your muscles and push the baby."

When the next contraction came, Rachel called out.

"Okay, push." Samantha pushed with all her might. "Keep pushing." Samantha sucked in her breath and used every ounce of strength she could muster. "Okay, relax, when the next contraction comes do the same thing."

Three more contractions came and Samantha gave it all she had. She pushed until her body felt entirely depleted. When Rachel asked her to push again, Samantha broke down crying.

"I can't! I can't! I can't!" Samantha called out over and over again. The room swirled around her. She couldn't concentrate. It was almost as if she were floating.

From the doorway of the room, a woman burst in. Her long dark hair bounced as she ran to the side of the bed and took Samantha's hands in hers.

"Excuse me..." A nurse hollered over the noise. The woman turned to her.

"I'm this girl's mother." Said Lorna Stately, and then turned back to her daughter. "Samantha. It's your mother."

Samantha stopped protesting and looked at her mother. On the opposite side of the bed stood Marion, her mouth dropped open. There was only one way to explain what had just happened.

James. James had called Samantha's mother. And she had come.

"Mother?" Samantha asked, not believing what she saw.

"Yes. I'm here."

"I can't do it, Mom. I can't." Samantha cried and fell against Lorna.

"Yes, you can. And you will." Lorna stated as she brushed her hand against Samantha's fevered brow.

With renewed determination, Samantha pushed and pushed.

"Good! Good!" said Rachel. "Here it comes!"

Before Samantha knew it, the baby was there. She lifted her head and caught a glimpse of the child as the doctor cut the umbilical cord. Then, before she could protest the baby was against her chest.

"It's a girl!" Samantha heard. She looked the child up and down. A beautiful, beautiful little girl!

The baby opened her eyes narrowly, and then shut them against the bright light. Samantha hugged the little body as tight as she dared and looked up at her mother.

Her mother! How had she known?

Samantha looked to Marion.

Marion's eyes brimmed with tears as she watched Samantha hold her child. She thought back to the day she had born her first little girl, the child she had given up. She hadn't been able to hold her. She only caught a glimpse of the little girl from across the room as they cleaned her up. A mess of dark hair topped off the little pink body.

Samantha's child had dark hair.

Suddenly a feeling enveloped Marion. She felt warm and comforted, like all the pain she had harbored for so many years had been erased. Marion marveled at the feeling. In her heart she praised God. He had finally saved her from the awful guilt. Helping Samantha had brought the closure that Marion had never been able to find elsewhere. He had finally given her a way to forgive herself. She looked up at Samantha and then at Samantha's mother.

A strange wave of recognition flowed through her body. She wasn't sure what it meant. Whatever it was, Marion knew that she was in the right place. God had sent Samantha to her.

CHAPTER NINETEEN
The Book
Hours Later

Marion and Lorna sat on either side of Samantha's bed and talked. Samantha was tired, but she didn't want to sleep. She didn't want to miss time with her mother.

"Thank you for taking care of Samantha." Lorna said to Marion.

Marion had wondered if she would have hard feelings towards this woman. Samantha had talked of so many problems at home. Marion expected something completely different that what had appeared in the hospital room today. Lorna looked much younger than she was. Her brown hair and brown eyes were healthy and full of life.

"You look great, mom." Samantha said to her mother.

"Thank you." Lorna paused for a moment. "I've been sober for seven months." The gravity of what her mother said, hit Samantha hard.

"Seven months?" Lorna nodded. Samantha realized what that meant. Her mother had stopped drinking after she had run away. Tears came to her eyes.

"Thank you, Mom..." Lorna pulled Samantha into an embrace.

A noise from the doorway pulled the two of them

apart. James stood there with his hands behind his back. There were tears in his eyes.

"James! Come in and meet Lorna." Marion waved him in. He approached the bed slowly his shoes squeaking against the linoleum floor.

"I talked to you on the phone." Lorna stated.

"Yes, that was I." James said with emotion.

"How did you find my parents phone number?" Samantha asked. She knew she hadn't given it to him.

James hesitated for a moment.

"You'll have to forgive me, Samantha. I went through your backpack. There was a book in there. Inside the front cover was a paper with your family's address and phone number. I felt impressed to call." His voice broke with emotion and he cleared his throat.

"What is it? What's happened?" Marion jumped up and went to his side. James hardly ever cried.

James could not speak. He looked from Samantha, to Lorna, and finally to his wife.

"I have one more confession, Samantha. I read the book that was in your backpack and I brought it here today."

Everyone looked at James in confusion. From behind his back, he pulled out a worn red leather book. The edges were worn.

Lorna's gasp was followed by a gasp from Marion.

"Samantha! You took my book! I thought I had lost it!" Lorna stood up and took the book from James's hands. She cradled it in her hands, with tears in her eyes. "I thought I would never see this again. It's the only thing I have that belonged to my biological mother."

"I only wanted to take something of yours with me, something you loved." Samantha said.

Lorna and Samantha noticed the look on Marion's face at precisely the exact moment. Her skin was white, as if she had seen a ghost.

Marion couldn't believe what she was seeing. It couldn't be! If that was what she thought it was, then... It couldn't be possible! She looked at James with wide eyes.

"You read it?" Marion asked James softly.

"Yes, I did." James replied just as softly. Currents of emotion flowed between them.

"Is that what I think it is?" Marion gulped.

"Yes, Marion, I think it is." James said gently. Marion's eyes filled with tears. She looked at Samantha. Then she looked at Lorna. The tears brimming her eyes now fell in silent streams down her flushed cheeks. She couldn't take her eyes off Lorna. One look at this woman and her daughter should have told Marion all she needed to know. But the book... the book was proof.

"What is going on here?" Lorna demanded holding the book closer to her. "Have you read it too?" she asked Marion.

"No. I haven't read it. I haven't seen it for years. But, I can tell you every word written in the first half of those pages." Marion said through sobs.

"What?" Lorna tried to grasp the meaning of Marion's words. "How do you know that?" Samantha watched Marion intently. She couldn't believe what was happening!

"Because I wrote it. And my mother wrote in it before me." Marion said and looked directly at Lorna.

CHAPTER TWENTY
Found
Moments Later

"What's going on?" Samantha asked. Her mother and Marion just stood there, looking at one another. James stood to the side with tears streaming down his face, his hands clasped together.

Marion turned to Samantha and began to explain.

"I've told you about the baby I had and gave up for adoption." Samantha nodded. "My mother gave me a book where she had written about me the day I was born. She wrote her hopes and dreams and how much she loved me. So, when my first baby was born I took that same book and wrote in it, just like my mother had. I wrote how I felt the day I had her. I told her how much I loved her and why I was giving her away." Marion looked up at Lorna. "I told her how much I wanted to hold her little body against me, and how I longed to keep her with me. But that I knew she would have a better life with a family who could give her what she needed. I gave the book to the adoption worker who said she would give it to the people who had adopted my baby. "

Now Lorna was crying, too.

"That's exactly what it says..." Lorna's voice trailed off as she realized the truth.

"I made a small list of names that I thought I would have liked to name her..."

"Deborah, Audrey, Francine, and... Samantha..." Lorna finished for her and put her hands over her mouth as Marion nodded.

"Marion?" Samantha asked, grasping at what this revelation meant.

"Samantha, the night I found you I was awakened by a feeling that I regularly have when one of my children have needed help. I've always had a special connection to my children. Never before had I been warned of danger when it concerned a stranger. Now I understand. Although you seemed like a stranger, you really weren't." Marion broke down in sobs

"What Marion is trying to say is this," James intervened. "Samantha, Marion is your grandmother." He turned to Lorna. "Mrs. Stately, you are the daughter that Marion gave up all those years ago."

Lorna went to Marion and stood before her, then with all the longing the years had brought they embraced. Tears streamed from their eyes and Marion dropped kisses on Lorna's cheeks. After a few minutes they drew away from each other and Lorna addressed Samantha.

"I named you Samantha because it was one of the names my mother had chosen. The day you were born I wrote in the book too, just like my mother had, about how I felt. It's fitting that you took it, considering the circumstances. I had planned on giving it to you when you had your first child. Since I couldn't find it I bought you another book."

She reached into her handbag and produced a beautiful leather bound journal. She handed it to Samantha.

"Write in it and give it to your daughter, so she will always have a little piece of you, like I had." Lorna said and looked into the eyes of her 'real' mother.

"You're saying that if I had never gotten pregnant and run away than we never would have found you?" Samantha asked Marion.

Everyone was silent for a minute, realizing the chain of events it had taken to bring them all to this point.

"God doesn't reward us for our mistakes." James finally broke the silence. "But he does use them to teach and to heal if we are willing to let Him. I'm sure that God would have found a way to reunite you all if this hadn't happened the way it has. Sometimes the hardest and darkest times lead us to the light. I do believe that this might have never happened with out you Samantha."

More tears fell and more embraces were shared.

"I feel as if a part of me that's been lost for so long has been found." Marion told Lorna through her tears.

"I do believe you've all been found." James's voice resonated through the room.

EPILOGUE
Aftermath

"Samantha, this has been one of the best Christmas' I have ever had." Lorna said softly as her and Samantha bedded down in the Mahoney's guest bedroom. There were two twin beds and two matching dressers. Above each bed were beautiful paintings of Christ.

Samantha agreed with her mother. It had been a wonderful Christmas. But for Samantha there had been something missing. She could not stop thinking about her baby.

Samantha and Lorna hadn't gone home to Connecticut. Lorna had called her husband from the hospital to let him know what had happened and that they would not be home until New Year's.

The days leading up to Christmas had been filled with preparations, shopping, getting to know James and Marion and their four children. Lorna had grown up as an only child. And with that came all the wishes only children had. She wished for siblings. Growing up, her friends had told her she was lucky. Sisters and brothers were only bothers. But Lorna couldn't see it that way. She had fantasized of the friendship she would have had if she had only had a sibling. Boy or girl, it didn't matter. Now, suddenly she had four. Two sisters and two brothers.

"Yea, mom. It's been great." Samantha said with less enthusiasm than Lorna had expected.

"Samantha?" Lorna asked with concern in her voice. She sat up in bed. Samantha sat in the bed across from her with her knees drawn up close against her.

"Have you ever given up something that you wanted more than anything in the world?" Samantha asked in a small voice.

"Yes, I have." Lorna returned with a far off gaze in her eyes, but didn't elaborate.

Even though Samantha had tried not to become attached to the child that she had carried it hadn't worked. The baby was a part of her. The image of her little baby girl, naked and crying against her chest filled her mind. She had been so small and perfect. It was amazing to Samantha that something like that could have come from her. At that moment in the hospital room Samantha had allowed herself to think about keeping her, but only for a moment. Giving her up was the right thing to do, Samantha was sure of it. She recalled the warm feeling when she had chosen the couple that would be her baby's parents.

"Do you think I'll ever get to talk to her?" Samantha said with a tear in her eye.

"Only time will tell, Samantha. I never thought I would meet my mother and look, here I am staying in her house and building the friendship that I always wanted." Lorna took in a deep relaxing breath.

"But you had to wait so long..."

"Yes. I did." Lorna sat up in bed and looked at her daughter who had not yet lain down. "But it was worth it."

"I hope someday she'll think that." Samantha said with a shaky voice. "I don't want her to think I don't love her. At least she'll have the book from me. She'll know what I went through and why I did what I did. I just hope that her parents give it to her." Samantha ducked her head between her knees to hide that tears that began to fall uncontrollably. There was a moment of silence as Samantha cried and Lorna looked on, not sure what to do. Keeping the baby had crossed Lorna's mind as well. But the thought of rearing another child, or Samantha rearing a child didn't sit well. Adoption was the best answer. After all, it had been a good thing in her own life.

"I need to apologize to you Samantha." Lorna said, finally. Samantha raised her head and looked at her mother in confusion. Lorna went on before she said anything. "I've seen you struggle. I watched how your father treated you. I never did what I knew I should have. I wasn't a good mother."

"Mom..." Samantha began, knowing full well that her father had been just as mean to her mother.

"No. I should have stepped in and not allowed it." Lorna said. Her shoulders slumped a little. "I don't know how to make it better. But I'll figure out a way, I promise." Samantha looked at her mother and smiled supportively. Though Samantha loved her mother she did not put much stock into the words she had just heard. For years her mother had just stood by. But, that didn't make Samantha love her any less. They were both pawns in the game her father played. Samantha wasn't sure how her mother meant to right what had happened; in fact Samantha didn't think she could. There was a lot Samantha could say to her mother. Instead, she stayed silent. Reparation would have to come later.

Her mother didn't say any more. She just lay down and closed her eyes. Samantha wiped at her eyes and followed suit. She wasn't sure if there was anything she could say to her mother. She couldn't tell her it was all right. There were things that should not have happened.

For now Samantha would be happy that change was possible and that her mother was here for her. But more importantly she was happy the she believed there really was a God.

Until now God had been nothing Samantha had considered to be real. Then suddenly, He was real and she could feel him. She felt him in the wind that blew the snow flakes down to the ground. She felt him in the warm rays of sunshine that filtered through the window.

She knew it was He that had brought her to this point. He healed Grandma Marion's heart. He had brought the beginnings of healing to Samantha's mother. And He had given Samantha the tools on which to rebuild and live her life. She was nervous about going home. She would be starting all over and she knew it would not be easy. But she could do it.

Samantha wasn't sure what the future would bring. She only knew that she could face it in a way she never had before. She had found strength and worth in herself. She had found meaning to life. Someday she would have more children of her own and she would teach them what she had learned. And maybe someday she would have the chance to do the same with the daughter she had given up.

A smile formed on Samantha's lips as she drifted off to sleep. In her heart she felt that a day would come when she would see her daughter again. Until then, God would take care of both of them. She had been found, her mother had been found, Grandma Marion had been found; and someday a little adopted girl who had been taken home to Wyoming could be found as well.